Thomas Miller

Little Blue Hood

Thomas Miller

Little Blue Hood

ISBN/EAN: 9783337363307

Printed in Europe, USA, Canada, Australia, Japan

Cover: Foto ©Andreas Hilbeck / pixelio.de

More available books at **www.hansebooks.com**

LITTLE BLUE HOOD.

BY

THOMAS MILLER,

AUTHOR OF "THE CHILD'S COUNTRY BOOK."

ILLUSTRATED

NEW YORK:

JAMES MILLER, PUBLISHER.

779 BROADWAY.

1880.

CONTENTS.

— —

4   CONTENTS.

LITTLE BLUE HOOD.

CHAPTER I.

THERE was quite a crowd before the rich jeweller's shop in Piccadilly, and not more than two or three out of the whole assembly rightly knew what had happened. One said what he thought, another reported what he had heard, while a third boldly asserted that it was a robbery ; as a proof of which he pointed to the policeman stationed beside the shop door. Some looked at the empty landau, with its rich lining and spirited horses, on which the coachman kept a watchful eye, while the two footmen stood beside the carriage, looking very frightened, and speaking very low. At length a superintendent of the police came up at a sharp trot, and said to the footmen, "Where's the lady ?" The answer was, "Inside the shop ;" into which, without uttering another word, the superintendent entered. While he was inside the shop, the measured tramp of half-a-dozen policemen came sounding along the pavement, and after clearing the crowd from the window and the carriage, they drew up, as if awaiting further orders. They had not to wait long before the superintendent came hurrying out with a memorandum-book in his hand, exclaiming, "Quick ! let information be conveyed to all the stations. A child, about six, in a little blue hood, her hair in ringlets, of a gold color, and a small black and white dog, are missing. Tell Sergeants Moore, Ratcliffe, and Shaw, to get on horseback, and convey the information to every man on the beat within a mile round. I am authorized to give fifty pounds for the recovery of the little girl. Quick ! the lady left her in the carriage with her dog only a quarter of an hour ago. Let the cabs and omnibuses be looked after, the bridges watched, and every court and alley searched about the neighborhood." He then said to the coachman, "Remain here until I return. I am going to Scotland-yard ; when I come back, I have a few questions to put to those footmen. Your lady is too ill to return home at present." Saying which, he set off at a brisk trot, leaving only two policemen before the shop.

Soon after an eminent physician came rattling up in his carriage to attend the lady, who was too ill to be removed. He ordered the landau to return home, just as a messenger arrived from Scotland-yard, summoning the footmen to appear before the head commissioner of the police force.

The footmen "had no tale to tell ;" one of them, feeling very thirsty, had hurried off to get a glass of bitter ale. He might be gone two or three minutes, perhaps five : when he came back he stood talking to the coachman, never noticed the landau, as he left John beside it ; thought all was right.

John, the other footman, feeling tired, had sat down for a minute or so on the landau steps, which he had not put up after the lady entered the shop. Trot, the dog, stood reared up inside the landau, and kept tapping him on the hat with his forepaws, causing little Blue Hood to laugh. Saw a gentleman's servant he knew, went to speak to him, was not above a minute or so. When he came back, saw the landau door open, and felt sure the little lady had got out, and gone into the shop after her mother. She had done so once before, and nothing was said about it.

And that was all. When the lady came out of the shop, and found her daughter was not•in the carriage, and the footman told her she had gone into the shop, to which the affrighted mother hastened back, only to find that her golden-haired darling Little Blue Hood was lost: it was then that she sunk senseless on a seat, when there was soon great hurrying to and fro, and messengers sent in every direction through the length and breadth of far-spreading London.

----•----

CHAPTER II.

THE DOG TROT.

IT was only a few months before that the dog Trot had found a home with his pretty mistress, Little Blue Hood ; and this was how it happened. She was sitting in the carriage waiting for her mother, when she heard a dog yelping and howling loud enough to be heard a quarter of a mile down Oxford street, and asking the footman what was the matter with the poor dog, was answered that "he had only been run over," and when he came and drew himself up, under the carriage, as if he knew what a kind heart there was above him, Little Blue Hood pleaded for him so piteously, that the servant took him very cautiously by the back of the neck, and lifted him into the carriage. When her mother returned, she found Trot, as ugly a little mongrel as ever ranged the streets, coiled up in Little Blue Hood's lap, and licking her hand. The wheel had only gone over his poor bit of a tail, so that he wasn't so very much injured; and never in this world did a dog display more affection to its preserver than Trot did to Little Blue Hood, while she loved him with all her heart.

Now, Trot had several times jumped out of the carriage as soon as the door was opened, as if he wanted to stretch his legs, but had always come back again after having had a bit of a run; for he quite enjoyed giving the footmen a breathing, and seemed to know that they would soon be after him, though when once again within the reach of Little Blue Hood's voice, he needed but a word from her, and was coiled up at her side in a moment, as if nothing at all had happened. But for his ugly, old-fashioned head, he would appear at times like a real gentlemanly dog, as if all his life he had been brought up to take his airing in a carriage, instead of hunting up and down all kinds of low streets, as he had done many a time, after a bone or a crust. But though he so often stood with his paws resting on the carriage door, let there only be a stoppage, and another dog at the door or window of the opposite carriage, then he would show his low breeding, by beginning to bark and growl, and displaying all his sharp white teeth, and it was only by pulling him down and shaking her little hand at him, that Little Blue Hood was able to make peace; and one day he jumped bang into an open carriage that came too near to please him, and began fighting a French poodle, and there was a pretty to do under the old lady's large crinoline, while they fought in the carriage. Also, when they got out for a walk in the park, he would sit down and scratch himself anywhere, or before anybody, while a real gentlemanly dog would have carried his fleas home with him into his kennel, and have punished them there, however much they might have worried him, rather than have had it thought that he kept such low-company, when in the presence of well-bred dogs and fashionable people. Also, if he saw any low-bred dog he would run up to it, wag his tail, and appear delighted to meet him, seeming to say, "Never mind, old fellow! I was once as poor and cast-down as you are, but you may yet live to ride in a carriage some day, as I do; so cheer up. I wish you had a few of those bones I have left unpicked at home. If you come round our way, give me a bark, and I'll get you in somehow and give you a meal;" for into some such droll language as that would Little Blue Hood interpret the expression of Trot's looks to her mother, for the child's head was filled with romantic ideas about all kinds of dumb animals. Nothing seemed to delight Trot more than having a fight in the park with some proud, stuck-up, clean, gentlemanly dog, that seemed to despise the very ground he trod upon; to fly at such a dog, and roll him in the dust, was often only the work of a few seconds, when, if attacked or pursued by the servants, who had charge of the other dog, Trot would run up to Little Blue Hood, and in her dear arms find safe protection. Nay, so polite were some of the ladies, and she so little and pretty, that they would throw all the blame on their own dogs, while that rascal, Trot, hid his ugly head under the long lappets of her little blue hood, and fairly grinned again

as he thought how well he had got out of another row.
But one day "he caught a Tartar," got his ears well bit,
and was a good dog for a week or two, his little mistress nursing him until he got well, when he broke out
again worse than ever ; so that at last she was compelled
to keep him within bounds by a long blue ribbon,
which she fastened round his neck, and held fast in her
hand when they walked. Now and then he made a tug,
and gave a spring ; but a jerk, and "Oh, fie, Trot!"
brought him back to subjection.

At one time or another there was no doubt but that
Trot had formed part of the establishment of some itin-
erant show-man, street-tumbler, or Punch-and-Judy-man,
for he could perform all such tricks as are generally taught
dogs in that kind of profession. He could walk about
on his hinder legs, upright as a grenadier ; stand on his
forelegs ; tumble ; lie down and pretend to be dead ;
carry a stick between his paws ; dance, after his fashion ;
and even sing, if a strain of low, whining barks can be
called by such a name. All these accomplishments were
discovered by Little Blue Hood before the end of a month,
and he would go through them all at any time at her bidding. Never had such laughter rang through that great
grand west-end house, as was raised by Little Blue Hood,
and her dog, Trot. True to his old habits, he would get
into the kitchen every now and then, where the cook
seemed almost to have as much command over him as
his little mistress ; and there he would sit up and beg,
holding some delicate morsel on his black nose, until some
number, told to him beforehand, was counted, when he
threw it off and caught it before it fell on the floor.
These tricks made him a great favorite with all the ser-

vants, and if he didn't get fat, it was not through a want
of good living. Trot displayed such a social disposition
when at home, that he was on friendly terms with the cat,
and they would lie on the fleecy rug for the hour together; even the parrot would now and then fraternize
with him, though there was always something of a ma-
licious leer in Poll's eye, as if she were thinking of their
first fight, when he laid hold of her by the tail, and left
only the stump behind, though she commenced the battle
by biting his poor ear.

"Ay, we shall all greatly miss the dog," said the footman, as they talked over the events of the day in the
kitchen;—a few hours after the little girl was lost.

"Not so much as my Lady will our dear Little Blue
Hood," said the tender-hearted, fat cook, bursting into
tears.

CHAPTER III.

THE LITTLE BLUE HOOD.

HOW Edith,—for that was her real name,—came to be
called Little Blue Hood, was through the fancy she
took to a silk hood, of that color, her dear mother had
made for her, just after she was strong enough to run
alone about the large, beautiful garden. It was a hood
and cape, all in one, and long enough to keep the sun
off her pretty neck and shoulders, having a ribbon run
into a hem, which sometimes was tied under her dear little

dimpled chin. She could not bear a bonnet, it pricked
her tiny pearl-like ears ; as for a hat, she was always
pulling and dragging at it, and twisting it into all manner
of shapes, throwing both off the moment she was out of
sight, then running in-doors to ask for her little blue
hood. She took it off, and put stones in it, then dragged
it up and down the broad gravel walk for a cart : she
made a carriage of it, and put her little white kitten in
for a ride, though after a jolt or two pussy always jumped
out, and preferred walking on the grass border to such
a rough conveyance ; and she pulled up the flowers and
presented them to her over-indulgent mother in her little
blue hood. They bought her the costliest dolls, with
eyes and hair of every imaginable color, and dressed in
the very height of fashion ; but she never seemed to care
for them after the first few days, nor ever fell asleep so
soon as when she took into bed with her, for a doll, her
little blue hood. Then, when she wore it, it was large
and loose, and she could pop her pretty head in and out
of it as quickly as a little brown mouse can peep in and
out of its hole. From under her hood, her sweet face
looked out like a beautiful flower from its calyx ; and
her gentle eyes, half sly, half shy, seemed to hide themselves beneath it ; while it threw down a soft half shadow
over her face, mouth, fair forehead, and gave a darker
tinge to the upper part of her golden hair ; then as the
inside was lined with a warm, rich pink silk, the color
heightened the rosy blush of her healthy face, and when
she sat still she looked like a beautiful picture set in the
frame of her little blue hood. But the blue hood she
wore when she went out for a walk or a ride with her
mother, and which was always bordered with costly

lace, hanging as low down behind as a little cloak, she never cared to put on when in the garden, unless they received visitors ; for it was always one of her old blue hoods that she wore to romp and play in, to fold up and make a seat, on which she would sit and sing or repeat the pretty childish poems her mother taught her. Perhaps it was wrong in her fond mother to indulge her so much, and give way to her childish fancies, but then she looked so pretty, and was so comfortable and happy in her little blue hood, that it would have pained her dear heart had she not been allowed to wear it, and it was a very harmless whim after all. Then all the ladies and gentlemen declared that nothing became her so well as her little blue hood, and they were right; and a celebrated painter, who wanted a model for his picture of Titania and her fairies drew her sweet face for his Fairy Queen, seated on a bed of flowers and peeping from out her little blue hood. And so she was known, and so she was called by all the friends of her parents Little Blue Hood ; nor did the servants amongst themselves, or when she herself was only present, mention her by any other name than that of Little Blue Hood. And after Trot found a new home with her, and became her inseparable companion, visitors who called always inquired after Little Blue Hood and her dog.

CHAPTER IV.

THE OLD KIDNAPPER.

THE father of Little Blue Hood had formerly been an eminent counsellor with so large a practice that he could not at last accept half the briefs that were offered him. At the time his little daughter was missing, he held a very high legal office under the crown, and just before his marriage was knighted. During his practice at the bar, he held a brief for an old woman ; but his client had sworn to so many falsehoods in her attempt to recover a property to which she had not even a shadow of a claim, that he threw up his brief in disgust the moment he heard the opposite counsel's defence. From that hour the woman hated him, said that he had sold her cause and ruined her, and that she would have her revenge on him somehow, if even she had to wait for years. This bad woman had gone to his chambers several times, and made so great a disturbance, saying that she knew he was in when he was on circuit, that at last one of the clerks gave her in charge of the police, and she was sent to prison. The counsellor, on hearing of this, expressed his regret at what had happened ; and said an asylum would have been a more fitting place for the woman, as he did not believe she was at all right in her mind. In prison she nursed the thoughts of her revenge, was sullen and silent, and refused to see the chaplain, and when she came out was lost sight of. The charitable counsellor inquired after her in vain, for he was anxious to render her some little assistance.

Years passed away, and that bad-hearted woman grew older and worse, never losing sight all the time of the gentleman, who she said had ruined and imprisoned her. She saw him rise to his high position, heard the name of the titled and beautiful lady he had married, went to look at the large grand mansion in which they lived, and uttering some terrible threat, as she saw their carriage drive up to the door, shook her withered old fist at it. The counsellor would not have known her then, had she come close up and spoken to him, so much had she altered for the worse. Some find pleasure in doing good; others a wicked delight in doing evil. Some are naturally kind; others naturally cruel. The father of Little Blue Hood was always studying to do good. That bad old woman's mind was ever filled with the thought of doing evil. There was no doubt a touch of craziness about the old woman; but she still retained the same roguish cunning which long years before had so far blinded a clever solicitor, as to induce him, at a great loss, to undertake the recovery of the property already alluded to. She had many a time seen Little Blue Hood with her parents, had followed the carriage through many a square and street, and hung about the house in which she lived, both by day and by night, for many a long hour together, endeavoring to obtain a chance of stealing her. She carried a folded bonnet and an old cloak to disguise the child the moment she saw a chance of seizing her, and thought how if she once got them on, she might cry and scream as loud as she liked, for she had excuses enough in her wicked old head to answer any questioner they might chance to meet.

The time came at last. Little Blue Hood pushed open the door of the carriage, and out Trot jumped; seeing the steps down, she descended, and ran after her dog. Trot made his way up in an inn yard, under the archway of which the wicked old woman was watching. There was no one about the yard ; the cloak and bonnet were thrown over the child in an instant, though not before the dog had bitten her hands. The old woman made a stab at Trot with a long pair of sharp scissors she carried in her huge pocket, but missed him. "Oh, do not hurt my poor dog," said the little girl, "and I will not cry nor make a noise."

"Take him up in your arms then," said the savage old woman, "and come along with me ; and if you look at, or speak to any one, or make the least noise, I will kill your dog."

And so Little Blue Hood was led along, stifling her sobs for the sake of her dog, which she carried under the old ragged cloak, while the wicked old woman gripped her tightly by the wrist.

CHAPTER V.

THE LARGE HOUSE.

WHAT a change had taken place in a few days in the home of Little Blue Hood! The blinds were drawn down, the great knocker was muffled, and cartloads of tan laid down on that side of the grand square to deaden the sound of passing vehicles. Those who came and went on necessary errands to the silent house, moved with noiseless steps and spoke very low, for the lady inside was ill, well-nigh unto death, and from no quarter had any tidings come to console her, as nothing had either been seen nor heard of Little Blue Hood or her dog.

Scores of pounds had been spent in advertisements, and thousands upon thousands of hand-bills circulated, offering as much as five hundred pounds for the recovery of the child, and a large reward for even any tidings of her, but no true tidings came, although there were many attempts to obtain the reward; but the father of Little Blue Hood was too shrewd a lawyer to be easily imposed upon, and had a way of his own of getting at the truth, by asking a few plain questions. He felt the loss of his darling daughter as much as his lady did, but as he said, "It will not do for me to give way too much, for inquiries must be made and not a stone left unturned; and these things will never be done properly if I give up, and only sit brooding and mourning over the loss of our little angel."

Several little girls had been found with light hair, and brought to the large house under pretence that they were lost, and with a hope on the part of those who brought them that they would at least receive some little reward; but as these made their entrance and exits down and up the steps of the area, they caused no disturbance in any other part of the mansion. Amongst these were one or two dear little motherless girls, who looked as if they came from very poor homes; while the women who brought them seemed rather anxious about being rewarded for the trouble, as they called it, though a hearty meal, and a few shillings distributed by the footman, sent them away satisfied. Yet they no more resembled Little Blue Hood than a lighted rushlight resembles the evening star. There was hardly a little girl lost for ten miles round London, but what was picked up and brought

2

to the large house in the square. "Oh! bother 'em," said the cook; "to think of that low washerwoman bringing that dirty little girl, that looked as if its face had not been washed nor its hair combed for a week or more, and wanting to persuade us that it was our dear Little Blue Hood, and that we should see the likeness in a minute, if we only washed her and put on nice clean clothes. A woman the other day brought a little girl with hardly a rag to her back; but bless her little heart, it wasn't the child's fault; and I did give her some of Little Blue Hood's old frocks and things that had been laid aside for dusters."

Many who went by turned to look at the large house or pointed towards it, while they spoke in whispers, mentioning the many thousands that Little Blue Hood would have inherited some day, and wondering whom it would go to if she never returned, for her father had married one of the wealthiest heiresses in England.

And now that beautiful lady, hot with fever, and writhing under an aching heart, was laid on her restless bed, finding no sleep but what was produced by taking strong opiates—a sleep which brings no rest—and in which she fancied at times that she was with her golden-haired darling, and that they were toiling along together, hand in hand, over dreary and dusty roads to which there seemed to be no end. And sometimes in this feverish sleep they seemed to be separated by a deep dark river, on the banks of which they stood in a dim kind of twilight, beckoning one another to cross; and then hideous faces appeared to rise above the water, and she would awake frightened, and begin feeling about with her hands, as if for something she had lost.

The portrait of Little Blue Hood was now brought into her chamber, and so placed that she could see it, when she turned on her side in bed; and when free from pain, she would lie and look at it for the hour together, until the smile on that pretty face seemed to brighten, and the light in those dear eyes became so fixed and intense, and full of hope, that the portrait almost seemed to speak to her, bidding her not give herself wholly up to despair, for they would live to meet again, and be clasped in one another's arms. And now and then, after such a revery, she would doze away a few minutes tranquilly, and instead of stumbling along dark, wild, troubled ways with her child, fancy they were sitting together among flowers in the sunshine, listening to the murmuring of pleasant streams, and the singing of sweet birds, and when she awoke she would weep to find it was only a dream.

That large house, so filled with joyous noise when Trot and his little mistress came bounding in out of the garden, the one barking and the other shouting, singing, or laughing, while the deep well-staircase echoed back the sound, and the parrot screamed to join them, and the pretty canaries began singing in their cages; that large house had now lost its cheerful voice, and the only sounds heard in the upper rooms were low whispers.

The servants moved about almost as noiselessly as if they walked with feathered feet, and not a door creaked on its hinges, when either opened or shut.

There were policemen outside, and no cry of busy trade was permitted to break the silence of that large square, every resident of which respected the gentle lady, and had at one time or another, exchanged a kind greeting with Little Blue Hood and her dog inside the green inclosure. Even the poor gardener, who attended to the shrubs and flowers in the square, came morning after morning to the area steps, to inquire if any thing had been heard of Little Blue Hood. "Bless her heart alive," said one of the gardeners, an old, gray-headed man, "it used to cheer me up as much as a pint of beer does, when I am very tired, and very thirsty, to hear her pretty tongue rattle along, saying such droll things at times, and making her dog do such pretty tricks, that I fairly laughed again. How we all do miss her, surely. I wish she had only been left to run about your own garden, or trusted to our care in the square, she would have never been lost—never been lost. But God tempers the wind to the shorn lamb." And many another as humble as the poor old gardener, came to the large house daily to inquire after Little Blue Hood and her dog.

------◆------

CHAPTER VI.

THE OLD WOMAN'S HOME.

WITH the large old flapping bonnet hiding nearly the whole of her dear sorrowful face, and the long shabby cloak concealing her dress, Little Blue Hood was dragged along by the old woman over Westminster Bridge, and into the New Cut, long before any information of her loss had reached the police stations in that locality. Though her little arms ached, and she was compelled to put Trot down, the faithful dog stuck to her as close as her own shadow. Scarcely a head was turned to look at the old woman or child, as they passed along this poor neighborhood, and made their way into one of the back streets; so much were they dressed like other women and children, with which the narrow pavements swarmed.

They could hardly get along, so much was their path encumbered by the vendors of fried fish, whelks, baked potatoes, and vegetables—the refuse of which littered every few yards they traversed, while bundles of wood and lumps of coal projected from the entrance of open sheds, and compelled them every now and then to turn out of the footway.

They passed along streets where half the tumble-down houses were empty, and those that were inhabited had never been painted for years, the wood-work looking like gray, dry bones round the window-panes.

And in these poor streets lived sweeps and night-men—men who spent their days underground flushing the sewers, coster-mongers and their donkeys, with their wives and children—all under the same roof; and others who got their living by disreputable means, when they were out of prison. Those who lived in the same house often knew nothing of one another, as each family or individual, renting a separate room, had their own keys, paid their rent to the collector, who came round once a week, and required only a week's notice if they wanted to leave. The tenant of one room did not know how the occupier of the next got a living; and very often they did not even know one another's names.

Some went out early of a morning, and returned late at night, and it was the business of no one to inquire whither they went, nor whence they came. Now and then, if a glimmer was seen through some chink at night, and some one came in, in the dark, and could not find a match, a light might be asked for, which was often only given by a hand through a narrow opening of the door, and saving when they went to the water-butt at the back, or to hang a few rags in the yard, that was all they saw of one another, sometimes for weeks together.

As for the old woman, she spoke to no one, nor made neighbors of anybody. Once she was ill, and a little girl came to attend on her; but she received orders to speak to no one, and obeyed. She was the daughter of an old servant, who had lived with the old woman in her prosperous days.

Even now she was not without money, though the sum was small, and when that was gone she knew not where she could obtain another shilling. There was only another tenant in the four-roomed house in which she occupied an apartment, and he was employed on the roads, and, excepting on a Sunday, never hardly came home in the day-time, so that half the house was empty, like many others in that poor neighborhood.

If any one did turn to notice the old woman and child enter the house, they took Little Blue Hood for the child who had been with her while she was ill, who was very little of her age, though nearly three years older than pretty Edith.

Trot made himself at home at once, by coiling himself up on the little morsel of carpet that covered the hearth; while Little Blue Hood seated herself on a hassock, which the old woman dusted before she let the child sit on it, for every thing in her room was clean.

The child watched her, as she took a bundle of wood out of a cupboard in which she also kept her coals, and lighting her fire, placed the kettle on it. Nor was it until the fire had burned up and warmed the apartment, that she took off the old cloak and bonnet, then taking a little dark frock and other things out of a drawer, she aired them well before the fire, and said, "You must wear these now. I have kept them a long time for you." And she took off her little blue hood and frock, and dressed her like a poor person's child, Trot looking on all the time, but neither barking nor growling, for the tears his little mistress shed, fell in silence, and when she was dressed he jumped up and sat on her lap.

Her heart was too full, and she had no appetite to partake of the tea the old woman made; but Trot began to beg as soon as he saw the bread and butter; but she shook her head, and said "No;" then pointed to her hand where he had bit her.

"He will never do so again," said Little Blue Hood. "Let him have my tea, he's hungry."

Without replying, the old woman handed her the plate of bread and butter; and after he was satisfied, and had lapped some milk and water, he began to tumble and dance on his hind legs, as if to cheer up his pretty mistress.

The eyes of the old woman lighted up as she sipped her tea, and watched the child and dog, for the thought entered her head in a moment, that, after a little practice, money might be obtained through their performance; and she muttered to herself, "Her father was the cause of my ruin, and I will make her and the dog support me; that shall be my revenge."

The day wore on; the evening began to close in; there was no pleasant square to look over and watch the sunset, no long garden to give her dog a run in before she went to bed, for the blind was drawn down, and she only saw the day darken by watching the deepening shadows on the walls, until at last she fell asleep with the dog in her arms.

At length, the old woman undressed her, put her on a clean little night-gown and cap, and drew down the bedclothes. Little Blue Hood stood still for a moment, with her bare feet on the floor, and said, "Please, I haven't said my prayers."

"Then say them to yourself," replied the old woman, sharply. "I never say mine."

So Little Blue Hood knelt on the narrow strip of carpet beside the bed, and with clasped hands, whispered her prayers; while Trot sat close beside her, never once moving until she arose, when the old woman had no sooner drawn the clothes over her than he jumped upon the bed, and coiled himself up between the wall and his little mistress.

"I shall not have the dog on my bed," said the old woman, angrily; "he must sleep on the floor."

"He will be as still as a mouse," said Little Blue Hood, "and never stir all night if I have my arm round him;" and she kissed the dog as she folded her arm round him, and felt that she was not yet wholly friendless.

The old woman attempted to drive him off the bed, but saw that he would fly at her if she persisted, so sat down and left him undisturbed.

So Little Blue Hood lay, her cheeks wet with tears, repeating the prayers to herself, with Trot folded in her arms, until sleep sealed up her gentle eyes; and she dreamed that she was hanging around her mother's neck, and fancied in her sleep that she was singing to her.

CHAPTER VII.

THE DISGUISE.

THE old woman folded up neatly the whole of the clothes the child wore when she stole her, and placed them carefully in a drawer, pinning up separately the little blue hood in a clean paper. Those she was to wear on the morrow she also folded as neatly, and placed on a chair, then sat down with her elbows resting on her knees, and her hands supporting her chin, and gazed motionless into the fire. There the old woman sat brooding to herself, and revolving in her mind what she should do to prevent the discovery of the child, well knowing that a great reward would be offered, and that hundreds of people would be out on the search for her in every direction.

"I will dye her hair black," said the old woman, to herself, "and stain her neck, face, and hands with the juice of walnuts, until she is as brown as a gypsy child, and her own mother would not be able to recognize her, unless she was very near, and heard her voice. She shall hold the dog, and every white patch about him I will also dye; then they may offer their rewards for their fine child with golden hair, and a black and white dog, and I will read the bills while they are standing beside me.''

Then she rubbed her skinny hands together over the fire, as if delighted at the wickedness she had plotted, feeling satisfied that it would almost be impossible to detect Little Blue Hood and her dog under such a disguise.

In the morning, the old woman went out noiselessly and purchased the necessary ingredients, and returned by the time the child awoke, bringing with her some meat for the dog, which Trot devoured with great relish, then wagged his tail for more. Little Blue Hood thanked her for being so kind to her dog, and as she brought her a hot French roll, sat down and made a hearty breakfast.

"I shall always be kind to both you and the dog,'' said the old woman, "while you do every thing I wish.'' But if you cry, or want to leave me, or ever speak to anybody when we are out, I will send away your dog, and as for you''—she looked at the child and said, " you will learn to love me.''

Little Blue Hood submitted to have her hair dyed, and her fair face and arms stained without a murmur; and as for Trot, he lay quietly in her arms, and never attempted to escape when she shifted him, while the old woman applied the brush to every part where there was a speck of white. As the dye dried up in a few moments, it neither endangered the health of the child or the dog; and after being applied two or three times, the hair of both was of a raven blackness, while the skin of Little Blue Hood was of a rich, deep olive.

On the fourth day, the old woman went out fearlessly with Little Blue Hood and her dog for a walk around the neighborhood; and in the shop windows, and on the

walls of the principal streets, saw the bills offering five
hundred pounds reward for the discovery of the little
girl she then held by her hand. "It is a deal of money,"
she thought to herself; "and I might get my old servant
to say she had found the child, and then keep out of the
way until she obtained the reward, and give her a por
tion of it, for but little would content her. But revenge
is sweeter to me than money, and her father threw up my
cause, then sent me to prison. Oh! the miserable hours
I passed within those walls. No; I will not be tempted
by the reward; keeping his child will give him the heart-
ache for many a long day, and that will be some consolation for what he has caused me to suffer. I wish she had
no mother alive, for her mother never did me any injury."

How new and strange did every thing appear to that
dear girl! She saw children but little bigger than herself
going of errands, and making purchases, haggling for a
farthing out of the dried rasher of bacon, picking pieces out
of the loaves, and drinking the beer they were taking
home; and when one barefooted child came running up,
and bit a piece off the end of her farthing sugar-stick, and
wanted to put it in her mouth, Little Blue Hood gave her
the penny the old woman had put into her own hand to
spend in whatever she might take a fancy to. The old woman told her she should not give her any more money to
spend if she wasted it in that way; then added a silent re-
buke, by going up to a cat's-meat shop and purchasing
some meat for Trot.

After questioning the child, the old woman found that
she knew several tunes, and could sing them in her pretty
way; and when once her little tongue was loose it ran on,
and she said, "I saw a little girl one day, no bigger than I

am, dancing and playing a tambourine, and Ma promised she would buy me one some day, so that I might play it and dance with Trot, and said she would teach me a many more tunes."

"If you are very good," replied the old woman, "I will buy you a tambourine to play on and dance with Trot; you already know plenty of tunes."

Little Blue Hood thanked her, and took hold of her hand kindly for the first time. A strange change came over the old woman's countenance as she took the child's hand within her own, and she felt something like a choking sensation before giving utterance to the falsehood that was on her lips, and then she said:

"Edith, do you know that I am your poor old grandmother?"

"My grandmother has been dead, oh! such a long while," replied the child; "and her picture is in the drawing-room. Ma often showed it me, and would sit still and look at it such a long time."

"But you had two grandmothers," said the old woman. Little Blue Hood shook her head, and then she knew that the falsehood she had told could not be detected by the child, and so she said: "That picture is the portrait of your Ma's mother. I am your father's mother and your other grandmother. Now you know why I have brought you to live with me."

The child sat silent, and full of thought for the space of a minute or more, then said, "Yes, you were very ill, and went where it was always warm, a long way off over the sea, and have come back again. But why did you not come to my father's; to those two pretty rooms, one looking over the square, and the other windows I used to see

from the garden, and which are always called grandmother's rooms?''

"Because I lost my money over the sea, and came back
poor," answered the old woman; "and knew your father
would not be kind to me. You would not be unkind to
your mother, would you, were she old and poor like me?''

"No; I should love her more, and give her all my money,
and all my toys, and I should——." But the tender heart
of Little Blue Hood was too full for her to say what more
she should do, were her dear mother old and poor, so she
burst into tears, and buried her pretty face in the old woman's lap. The wicked old hypocrite kept saying, "Don't
cry, dear, and break grandmother's heart," all the while
stroking her hair.

At last she took out her little handkerchief, dried her
eyes, and said, "Father loves me dearly. We will go
home; I will take you to your pretty rooms, play the tambourine dear mother will buy me, and Trot shall dance with
me, and father will love you because you are my grandmother, and you shall go with us in the carriage. Lock
the door, and let us all go now."

"Yes, we will some day," answered the old woman.
"But you must have your tambourine, and we will first
go out into the pleasant fields, where there are birds and
flowers, and you shall play and dance to me there. You
will like that, will you not?''

"I shall like it very much," replied Little Blue Hood
"because it will be like our large garden at home. And
this house is so dark, and there are no trees. When
shall we go?''

"As soon as you can play your tambourine," replied
the old woman; "I will buy you one to-morrow."

And so without a shadow of suspicion on the part of Little Blue Hood, she learned to dance and play the tambourine, to the great delight of Trot, and with a hope that she should soon be taken home by the wicked old woman, who by telling falsehoods had got her to believe that she was her grandmother.

CHAPTER VIII.

MAKING PREPARATION.

TROT had a gay little hat and coat made for him, which fastened under his throat and under his loins, and Little Blue Hood laughed, with something of her old merry home-laugh, the first time she saw him stand up to dance with her; he had such a droll look with his fore paws hanging down, and wore his new dress as if he had been used to it all his life, and didn't mind it at all.

He didn't know what to make of the tambourine at first, but he soon got used to it, and no sooner saw it in the hands of his little mistress, than up he jumped, and began bobbing about on his hind legs in a moment. The hat seemed to be rather in the way when he tumbled, and he was made to understand that when he commenced this part of the performance, he was to take it off, which he did very nimbly with his fore paws, and that was called "making a bow to the ladies," and no sooner were those words uttered by Little Blue Hood, than off went Trot's hat. Then he was taught to put the string behind his neck, and let the hat rest on one of his fore paws, and so carry it before him with the crown downwards.

Dainty bits were put into it for him to eat, as a reward, and he became so perfect that, when he was hungry, and could get hold of his hat, he would carry it before him and begin to beg, walking round the table on his hind legs.

Never was so perfect a little beggar made of a dog before, as Edith made of Trot, from hints given her by the old woman, and her own natural drollery; and often when after dancing she laid down her tambourine, he would give a merry "bow-wow-wow," which was his way of crying "bravo—encore."

There was something very graceful in her manner of dancing, in the way she threw back her pretty head, and raised her arms, while beating the tambourine, her long hair flying about with the motion, and her eyes sparkling again with delight, as she watched the strange antics of Trot, who looked as grave as an old monk while he went round and round, with his tail sweeping the floor, and his little hat falling off at times.

For the child, the old woman purchased several yards of muslin, to make her dancing frocks, and these she ornamented with spangles and other such like tinsel decorations; also buying for her pink silk stockings and little white boots, which contrasted strongly with her tawny face, neck, and arms, giving her quite a foreign look with her long hair now dyed a beautiful rich black.

She was soon perfect enough to beat time to her measured steps on the tambourine, and even Trot caught enough of the tune to move his hind legs more rapidly when she quickened the beat.

Bits of drapery had also been placed on the chairs, and as he moved from one seat to another, with his hat before him, he was taught to make a bow before each chair, which he did by shaking his head. Money was also dropped into his hat, and although he persisted for some time in taking whatever was put into it to his pretty mistress—unless it was food—he was at last made to deliver his hat to the old woman, who returned it after she had taken out the money.

"The ladies and gentlemen will put plenty of money in Trot's hat, to buy him meat with when we go out visiting," said the artful old woman, "and I shall save it all for him." And she never breathed a word to Little Blue Hood about their performance bringing in money for any other purpose, and she well knew that the affectionate child would do any thing, that laid in her power, for her dog.

What stories were told to win the affection of Little Blue Hood, after she got her to believe she was her grandmother, by that deceitful old woman, can hardly be conceived. She told the child that when she left England to go abroad for her health, she was only a little baby in long clothes ; and that she should never have brought her away, had not her father refused to let her see her after she returned.

And Little Blue Hood believed all she said ; for, never having told a wilful falsehood in her life, no such thought entered her innocent mind, as that her pretended grandmother was constantly telling her lies to win her pity and love, to serve her own wicked and selfish ends.

At last, the child began to think her father was very unkind to his aged mother, and this puzzled her very much, as he was so kind to everybody, and so charitable to the poor, and loved her so dearly. But the idea entered her mind, and the old woman deepened the impression she saw she had made, by adding falsehood to falsehood, until at last the child showed less regret at the thought of leaving her father, while her wish to see her dear mother was una bated.

Had she been older and able to reason, she would have sat down and recalled every thing she could remember in connection with her father's character, and would soon have convinced herself that the old woman's assertions were as false as if she had said that when the sun shone it made the earth dark.

Every necessary preparation had been made for some days, when one evening the old woman went out after tea, leaving the child to amuse herself with her dog, and promising to bring in something very nice for supper when she came back. She was gone a long time, and when she returned, she said, "You shall have your pretty frock on to-morrow, and I am going to give you a ride in a steam-packet, where you will see a great many ladies and gentlemen with their children, and you are to show them how beautifully you can dance, and all the tricks Trot can do. Will it not be pleasant?"

Little Blue Hood was delighted at the thought of such a pleasant trip. The boat was hired by a party of publicans for an excursion to Gravesend and back, and the old woman had obtained permission to show her little performance on board.

3

CHAPTER IX.

THE FIRST PERFORMANCE.

THE old woman, Little Blue Hood, and Trot were among the earliest arrivals, and took their places on a seat near the entrance of the best cabin of the steamboat, Trot hiding himself under the cloak of his little mistress, and poking his old-fashioned head out every now and then to see what was going on. The dog's hat and the tambourine were concealed under the old woman's cloak; his new jacket he wore, and the child had put on her dancing dress.

The excursionists soon began to arrive; the women were fine portly dames, expensively if not tastefully dressed; the children also were clean, healthy, and happy; while their husbands, having for one day left their bars to the care of their servants, looked as if they meant to enjoy themselves, and were altogether as fine a set of "jolly fellows" as ever the sun shone on. A few children from the Licensed Victuallers' School had, at the request of the landlords and landladies, who had known their parents, been allowed to join the excursionists; and no sooner did they come on board, than great packages of good things were thrust into their hands; and one smiling hostess, as big round as one of Barclay's beer butts, thrust a packet of Banbury cakes into the hand of Little Blue Hood.

Trot was out of his hiding-place in an instant, and begging with all his might; and a pretty clapping of little hands and "Oh mys!" there was when the children saw him, in his spangled jacket, performing all his wonderful tricks. Men and women began to cluster round, and the

children to climb on the seats; and when the old woman
said—"If they would clear a space round the deck they
should see her little granddaughter dance with her dog,"
the landlords began to put their laughing wives out of the
way as they would have done so many barrels that had
stood in the road of customers coming to their bars.

A gangway was soon made between the seats all round
the after-deck, and Little Blue Hood, slipping off her cloak,
and with such a courtesy as is never taught at schools,
shook the tambourine above her pretty head, while with
a footfall almost as noiseless as the dew falling on the fleece
of a sleeping lamb, she commenced dancing with a grace
that surprised the beholders, as much as the bobbing about
of Trot with his hat on delighted the children.

Even through the dye which stained her cheeks, a close
observer might have seen the color rise when she began
her first performance—that blush of modesty which caused
her to doubt her own ability for a moment, and was as sud-
denly lost in the loud shouts of applause that greeted her.
The old woman gazed on her in silent wonder; she had
never seen her do any thing like it before.

The smooth, spacious deck afforded ample room for her
graceful movements every way, while the fresh air from
the river, and the cheerful sunshine seemed to give her
new inspiration. Whichever way she looked presented
a new image of beauty. You could no more transfix her
airy steps, the motion of her arms, as she whirled the tambourine aloft, and her ever-varying and graceful postures,
than you could the twinkling of a sunbeam; for before
the eye had time to take in one position, it had changed to
something far more beautiful. She had been taught by
her mother, who, in the days of her maidenhood, was one

of the most graceful dancers human eye ever dwelt upon.

Trot also came in for his share of applause, and when he took off his hat and made a bow to the ladies there was such a clapping of hands as made the ears tingle again. Only to look at his droll countenance would have made a grave monk laugh over his prayers. Trot went round as he had been taught, with the string of his hat slung behind his neck, and the crown resting on one of his fore paws as he carried it before him, while walking upright on his hind legs, and received nothing but silver from his admirers; for the children were not allowed to contribute.

The publicans and their wives had come out to spend money, and parted with it freely—sixpences, shillings, florins, and even half-crowns, came tumbling into the dog's hat, until it was nearly filled. One good-natured landlord had no silver, so put in half a sovereign, intending to give two shillings for himself and his wife; but, no sooner did he attempt to take out of Trot's hat the eight shillings change, than the dog growled and showed his teeth, and placed his other paw over his hat to the great amusement of the lookers on.

"What a capital barman he would make," said one; "no money returned after it has once passed into the till;" and his brother publicans laughed again, until the landlord himself, who was the victim, joined in the merriment, saying, "Well, it's the first time I ever trusted to a dog to give me change; but remember, old fellow," speaking to Trot, "when you come to my bar, I shall expect you to stand a bottle of wine."

The old woman offered to give him back the change after she had emptied the well-filled hat into her capacious pocket; but this the publicans would not allow; for, as they said, "They had had fun enough for their money." Then, as they dropped the money into Trot's hat, they gave him bits of sandwiches, fowl, tongue, beef, sausage-rolls, and no end of other good things, with which they were well provided; for they began to eat and drink almost as soon as the boat was on her way, as many of them had not breakfasted.

But, if Trot was the favorite of the children, Little Blue Hood won the hearts of the wives of the publicans. Her beautiful features, modest manners, and low, sweet voice, as she replied to them with downcast eyes, made many a one wish, as they kissed her, that they had such a little darling to call their own, especially those who were childless. One wealthy wine-merchant came up, a plain, homely, kind-hearted man, and giving the old woman his card, said: "Look you here, missus, my wife's taken a strange fancy to your pretty granddaughter; and if you've a mind to bring her, and both of you come and live with us, we'll try to make you as happy as the days are long. She shall be brought up like a lady; and as we have no child, and as I am worth a few thousands, and we have nobody to leave it to but the school, we'll leave her well off when we are all dead and gone. Think it over, mother, and come any time; you shall both be as welcome as flowers in May."

He meant what he said. They had buried their only child when she was about the same age as Little Blue Hood, and the wine-merchant's wife fancied she traced a strange resemblance in our little dancer to her lost daughter. But it was only fancy.

Little Blue Hood and the old woman remained all day

with the excursionists, and she repeated her performance in the cabin, on their return in the evening, when it was too dark to remain on deck. The child had money given to her, which she was told to keep for herself; but on reaching home, she gave it all to the old woman, for she hardly knew the use of money, beyond giving it to the poor, as every thing had beforetime been purchased for her that her heart or her eye desired.

That night, while Edith was asleep, the old woman counted up the money for the first time, and said to herself, "A few such days as these, and we shall have no need to go trailing out in the cold, dark days of winter."

Perhaps she was thinking more of saving herself than of sparing Little Blue Hood; though, for the first time, she felt as kindly towards the child, while looking at the pile of money, as a cruel master does towards the donkey he has been beating all day, when he counts up the produce at night, and thinks he should not have been the possessor of such a sum, had it depended on himself, instead of his hard-working animal.

CHAPTER X.

MEETING AND PARTING.

LITTLE Blue Hood pined for the fresh air, the smell of green fields, and the wide-spreading sunshine—the gold of heaven which is dispensed alike to the evil and to the good—and which seemed imprisoned in the close courts and alleys of the old Borough, and beat its golden wings against the shattered casements and dilapidated door ways, as if to get away ; and after a day or two, the old woman gave her consent to the promised journey into the country.

She locked up her room, and taking a change of clothing for the child, entered the first Norwood omnibus that passed, concealing her bundle and the tambourine under her cloak ; while Trot, as if fancying that he was again taking his usual airing in the carriage, jumped upon the seat, and rearing up, amused himself by looking out of the open window of the omnibus, and barking at everybody they passed.

That morning the old woman was in one of her sullen moods, for there were times when, beyond a "yes" or a "no," she never spoke to the child for hours together : it may be, that during such intervals, the worm of remorse was gnawing at her conscience, and allowing her no rest because of the evil she was doing. Had a stranger seen those two faces in the morning sunshine, as they walked along the high road that looks over London on the one hand, and far away over the pastoral scenery of Surrey and Kent on the other, he would have been struck by the resemblance they bore to the personification of Good and Evil, as they have been pictured in all ages.

The sweet sunshine, the singing of the birds, the murmur of myriads of insects in the air, the long leaves ever making a low rustle, when stirred by the refreshing breeze, as if they were talking in whispers to one another, made the heart of the child glad ; and she began to carol snatches of little songs, which she had caught up from her dear mother, and which, to a listening ear, would have been the sweetest music of all.

In the countenance of the old woman there was nothing glad, nothing even hopeful, and as she looked at Little Blue Hood, it was with an evil eye, as if she not only envied, but hated her for being so happy: like those bad spirits who, consigned to the bottomless pit for the crimes they committed while on earth, sometimes rise to the surface, and catch afar off through the opening smoke and flame, dim glimpses of the golden battlements of heaven, and the white-winged ranks who stand there amid the surrounding glory.

Regardless of the white dust which curled up and drove before her, powdering all the wayside flowers, the child went singing along her way; while Trot, at one moment gave chase to a butterfly, and the next set off in pursuit of a bird, going over five or six miles of ground to every mile they traversed, barking and bounding, and jumping up to his little mistress, who often had a run with him over the green wastes that edged the dusty highroad with a border of grass and flowers. Sometimes, seeing the old woman so sad and silent, the child came alongside her and slipped her dear little hand into the other's palm, chatting away all the time to comfort her, or bringing her a few wild flowers to please her, until at last the old woman's stern brow relaxed.

"I'm sure the poor dog must be hungry," said the old woman, as they stood before a large mansion where several ladies and gentlemen were either seated on the smooth lawn, or pacing about the broad gravel walks and shrubberies. "Go inside with the dog, and I will come to you if they receive you kindly. Put on his hat and jacket, and give me your cloak; there is your tambourine. Don't be afraid; they'll no doubt give Trot a good dinner," and while she spoke she unloosed the child's hair, wiped the dust off her boots, and put the crumpled folds of her spangled frock into order.

At the first beat of her tambourine, there was a look of welcome in the countenances of the party before the mansion, as if they were glad of the change; for even pretty young ladies become as weary of hearing the same compliments, hour after hour, as gentleman do in uttering them, and the presence of Little Blue Hood and her dog was quite a relief, for one or two of the party were already yawning, and wishing it were time for luncheon.

It would only be a repetition of what took place on the steamboat to record the applause she won, and how well Trot acquitted himself, though this time she performed before a more discriminating audience.

"Were the child fair instead of dark," said one lady to another, "I should fancy it was Little Blue Hood, for she has just the same graceful action I have seen in that lost little darling, when dancing before her mother."

The old woman, who was standing behind her, heard every word she said, and was now as anxious to put a stop to the performance as she had before been for it to commence. But the gentlemen cried "encore," and the ladies applauded, without ever thinking how much such exertions in the hot summer sunshine wearied the pretty dancer. The master of the mansion, seeing that the child looked tired, ordered a servant to bring out wine, which he handed to Little Blue Hood himself; and when he found she preferred water, which was soon brought, and refused any refreshment for herself, but in her low, sweet voice, and with eyes cast down said, "I danced for you to give some dinner to my little dog," he patted her on the head, for he was fond of dogs, and ordered some cold meat to be given to Trot.

It takes very little to create a sensation, even amongst fashionable people, when they are moping in a country house; and Little Blue Hood, seated on the lawn, feeding Trot from a plate of cold roast beef, caused the ladies to gather round and admire her, and the gentlemen to apply their glasses to their eyes and exclaim, "Quite charming! a most interesting and beautiful child." Another, after stooping down and examining her through his glass, said: "A most singular and natural phenomenon: dark skin, black hair, and light-blue eyes: fine subject for Darwin in his *Origin of Species*."

Money had again been thrown by reckless if not generous hands into Trot's hat; and the old woman every moment became more anxious to get away, having reaped another good harvest, and becoming fearful, from the remarks already made, that questions might be put to her which would be difficult to answer, and lead in the end, perhaps, to discovering that she had stolen the child. This suspicion caused her to speak cross to Little Blue Hood, who was playing with the dog while she fed him, and making him do several little tricks which he had not before exhibited; until at last the old woman lost her temper, and taking the child by the arm, dragged her roughly away.

On one side of the mansion was a swinging gate, opening into a footpath that cut through the corner of a wood, if so small a space of ground, with its few remaining trees and undergrowth of wild shrubbery, may be called by such a name; though it was all that was left of what had been a large wood, only a few years ago, through which a railroad now ran, overlooking large spaces of cleared ground, that here and there were built upon.

They had scarcely got inside the gate, which Little Blue Hood was in the act of swinging back, as she stood with her face to the high road, when a carriage drew up with a slackening pace, as if its destination was the mansion they had just quitted. Little Blue Hood raised her eyes to look at the open carriage, and exclaimed, "Mother! mother!" throwing out her arms over the closed gate, as if to reach the lady in the carriage. At the selfsame moment of time the old woman also raised her eyes, and saw the father and mother of Little Blue Hood in the carriage; then seizing the child by the wrist, she said, hissing out the words through her clenched teeth, "Speak another word and I'll strangle you," plunged with her into the dense underwood, leaving far behind the cry and the shriek of "My child! my child!" uttered by the mother as she fainted away in the arms of her husband.

The owner of the mansion, a distinguished member of parliament, and an intimate friend of the father of Little Blue Hood, had persuaded him to bring his lady down for a day or two, for a change of air and to see his roses, which were then in perfection. Had she arrived ten minutes earlier, she would have seen her daughter dancing on the lawn.

When the mother of Little Blue Hood recovered from her swoon, and heard the remarks of the ladies and gentlemen who gathered around her, she was still of the same opinion, and in her own mind felt certain that it was the voice of her child she had heard. "Say what you will," she replied, "that voice pierced my heart. It might be a dream, for I think I was dozing at the time; but sleeping or waking, it was the voice of my lost darling that I heard.'' Her husband and the servants had also heard that cry of "Mother! mother!" but hers was the only heart it had reached.

Clear-headed as the father of Little Blue Hood was, and able to pick out a grain of truth from under a pile of falsehood, the thought that his child's skin might have been stained, and her hair dyed, never entered his mind. Then the dog was black too! and so one of the shrewdest lawyers in England was outwitted by a change so simple and easy, that a child might have done it, if supplied with the materials, as well as that treacherous and wicked old woman. He was ashamed to send out servants to search for them, after the evidence given by the company; and even the lady, who had remarked how much the dark child's dancing reminded her of Little Blue Hood, was convinced through the cross-examination of the clever lawyer, that there was no resemblance at all between the two; while the gentleman who noticed her beautiful light-blue eyes, almost began to think that they must have been as black as sloes, after he had been questioned by the child's father.

And how often do we meet with people like the father of Little Blue Hood who are too clever by half; and who, if told that you had seen a rainbow in the sky, would have argued for the hour together that you ought not to believe your eyes, unless you could prove what material it was made of. If, instead of displaying his skill in cross-examining his friend's visitors, he had sent out at once to search for the old woman and child, he would have recovered his daughter, and brought back happiness to the heart of his disconsolate lady, whose beautiful face had never been lighted up with a smile since the day she lost her dear Little Blue Hood.

---◆---

CHAPTER XI.

DEAF AND DUMB.

THE whole nature of that bad old woman, instead of having undergone a change, was now revealed in its true and hideous light, as clutching Little Blue Hood by the wrist, she dragged her through the dense underwood, regardless of the thorns and brambles that scratched and tore the arms and legs of the child, and which in her passion she herself did not feel at the time, though her wrinkled old limbs felt the pain afterwards.

Avarice was now added to her other evil motives for retaining the child, for the sums of money she obtained through her performance, trebled her most remote calculations. And then to think how near she was losing her, and how severe a punishment she must have received had the carriage arrived only one minute earlier while they had been on the open highroad. "I never thought of her voice," said the old woman to herself; "there is no staining or dyeing that. But in future, excepting when we are alone, she must appear deaf and dumb. I will make her do that."

When they arrived at an open space in the wood, the savage old woman said, "Sit down. What are you crying for?"

"Because I want to go to my mother, and you have hurt me with the sharp thorns," replied Little Blue Hood, while Trot reared up, and began to lick off the tears as they trickled down her cheeks.

"Have I not told you that when the time comes we will both go to her?" said the old woman. "The time has not yet come. You want to leave your poor old grandmother to go wandering about all alone, until she loses herself, and lies down somewhere to die where nobody will find her."

"I do not want to leave you," replied the child, "but to take you with me to my mother, and I am sure father will be kind to you."

"I hate your father," answered the old woman, savagely; "and would sooner see you dead and buried than let you return to him. Yes, buried alive; for I could not find in my heart to kill you."

"Buried alive!" exclaimed the child, looking at the old woman horror-stricken. "Oh! that would be very dreadful!"

"Yes; you would lie there covered up in a little churchyard," continued the old woman, "and nobody would know that you were there. You would hear the bells ring, and feel the shaking of the ground above you as the people walked over your grave to go to church; but they would not hear you, however loud you might shout. And there would be no light, nor any thing for· you to eat or drink, though you would be both hungry and thirsty; and would only have the dead outside you for company."

The child shuddered as she cast down her eyes, then said, "Oh, do not bury me alive. I will do all you tell

me, and be very good. I am not afraid to die, because I
say my prayers and shall go to heaven. But to lie in the
cold, dark ground alive and hear the bells ring and the
people all walking and talking above me in the sunshine,
would be worse than if you killed me with your sharp
scissors, as you said you would Trot;" and she drew
closer to the old woman, while she pleaded so pitifully,
trembling as she ventured to take hold of her wrinkled
hand.

"I love you too well to injure a single hair of your
pretty head," said the cruel old hypocrite, "and it is
only when I fear that I may lose you, that I seem to wish
you dead. Promise to obey me in every thing I may wish
you to do, and we shall soon return to your mother, never
to leave her any more."

"I promise to obey you in every thing," said Little
Blue Hood, "for I know you will not wish me to do any
thing that is wrong or wicked."

"Then hear me," said the old woman, fixing one of her
cruel looks on the child, "you must appear to be deaf
and dumb, never seeming to hear any thing, whatever
people may say."

The tears again fell like rain, and at last she said,
" But may I not talk to my dog ?"

"No, you must never speak at all," said the old
woman, "excepting when I tell you ; and that will only
be when there is no one by to hear you but myself. You
are to be the little deaf and dumb dancing girl. There,
you can talk to Trot now as much as you like, but after
we are out of this wood, you must not utter a single word
again, until I bid you speak."

Little Blue Hood took the food the old woman gave her

for her dinner, and went to the farthest side of the open green space, and there sat down under a tree, her heart too sad to allow of her tasting a morsel; and, as she fed Trot, who seemed always to be hungry, she stroked him, and said, "I am never to talk to you any more, Trot, only when we are by ourselves; but you will love me all the same, will you not? and know what I mean when I only look at you, and never leave me to run far away and be lost, because I must not call to you to come back again? No, you will be a good dog, and know that though I must not speak, I shall always be thinking of you, and dear mother and father, and home. And when we see dear mother again, we will run to her and jump into the carriage, and tell the coachman to gallop with us all the way home; for grandmother does not love us as dear mother does, who always liked to hear me talk and sing. And now kiss me; for I must not speak to you any more to-day."

Trot touched her dear face with his black nose, looking as if he understood every word she said, and a great deal more, for running to where there was an opening between the trees, he began to bark, as if he would have said, "Let's be off down here; the old woman can't catch us if we run our fastest; and I don't like her ways at all. I knew the horses the moment I saw 'em; for I've often had a sleep beside them in the stable. Come along, I'll run up to the door and give a bark, and your mother will soon come out. It isn't very far." And Trot ran some distance along the entangled footpath, as if to show her the way; then, finding that she did not follow him, came galloping back again.

When Little Blue Hood sat down beside the old wo-

man, and looked at her careworn and sorrowful countenance, her heart reproached her for entertaining for a
moment the thought of running away and leaving her,
and she said, "Never mind, if I see my mother, I will not
call to her, nor go away until you go with me; but will
be kinder to you than my father is, if you will love me."
And so saying, she laid her head down in the old woman's lap, and was soon asleep; for the long walk, and
dancing on the lawn, had wearied her.

The old woman answered not a word: though she
showed some little kindness in throwing a corner of her
cloak over the face of the child while she slept, to shelter
her from the noonday sun. Trot, also, coiled himself up
into a ball, and was soon sound asleep at the feet of Little
Blue Hood.

CHAPTER XII.

THE SILENT JOURNEY.

MANY a picturesque village and tranquil homestead did
they pass, in the course of the week they spent in wandering about the borders of Kent and Surrey; and the
old woman collected large sums at times, before respectable houses, for the performance of Little Blue Hood and
her dog.

She generally halted early in the evening, at any clean
quiet roadside cottage that took her fancy, always paying
liberally for the accommodation, on condition that she and
the child had a room to themselves. Many a dainty mor-

4

sel, which she shared with Trot, was given to that beautiful child ; and many a kind eye looked suspiciously on the old woman, and had their doubts about Little Blue Hood being deaf and dumb, through the changes they saw take place in her sweet face, when they asked questions about her ; to which, if the old woman made answer at all, she only told falsehoods.

Often was the child about to return thanks to those who were so kind to her and her dog, and the words would sometimes spring unaware to her lips, for hers was a most grateful heart ; but only in one or two instances did she forget herself, during the first and second day, and that happened at places where the old woman had not stated that she was deaf and dumb ; for unless questioned she rarely spoke a word. Her threats, after she had so far forgotten herself, so frightened Little Blue Hood, that at last she never opened her lips to utter a word, unless when the old woman told her she might talk. She saw numberless things in the green out-of-door world that she had never seen before, and wanted to know all about them, but her pretty lips were sealed, and she dare not ask a single question. The cattle lowed, the lambs bleated, the bees hummed among the wayside flowers, while the butterflies flew round and round as they played with one another ; and though sometimes she could not help pulling at the old woman's cloak, and pointing with her little finger for her to look, she kept her promise, and never spoke a word.

That sweet voice, which, to her mother's ear, made the most delicious music that ever filled it, was now hushed through awe of that cruel old woman, who would not allow her to give utterance to her feelings ; but dragged her along the dusty roads in silence, and so wrapped in her own thoughts at times, that however weary, hungry or thirsty, the child might be, she paid no regard to her.

Her little heart would have broken through sorrow at remaining silent so long, had she not now and then managed to run on beyond hearing of the old woman after Trot, and talked to her dog. If at such times a word or two caught the old woman's ear, she said nothing ; for it was only in lonesome and out-of-the-way places that she allowed Little Blue Hood to run after and play with her dog ; and in doing this, she had a selfish motive, well knowing that if she lessened the attachment which existed on both sides between the child and dog, they would not be likely to perform so well together.

Though the child had a brave little heart, yet there were times, when she danced on the dry white highways of the village streets, that the dust, raised by the rapid motion of her graceful steps, almost choked her, and made even Trot sneeze again ; but she pressed her dear lips tightly together, and as the kind-hearted village-women seldom failed in offering her a cup of milk, she drank, and tried to forget her troubles.

Often, when walking beside the old woman in silence, she repeated to herself the pretty prayers and little hymns her mother and her nurse had taught her ; and as she raised her blue eyes to the sky, fancied, at times, she saw white-winged angels bending over her in the forms of the silver clouds, and those seemed to be her great Comforters.

Sometimes they sat down and ate their noonday meal in the pleasant hayfields, where the wild roses were blowing all about the hedges, and the golden-belted bees buried their heads in the crimson-streaked flowers of the woodbine, while near at hand the tall scarlet foxgloves shot up like pillars of flame. And Little Blue Hood would gather trails of the pink convolvulus, and intermix them with the blue cyanus or cornflower, weaving between sprigs of the deeply-crimsoned pimpernel, and so making a wreath to bind about her hair, in which she would dance at times, until nearly every bloom had fallen out or faded. She had a fine natural taste of her own in arranging the various colors of wild flowers, and many a shilling found its way into the old woman's pocket when the child, with a graceful courtesy, presented her nosegays to the ladies, who often expressed their delight at seeing wild-flowers arranged so tastefully.

Trot's greatest delight seemed to be getting into a field where there was a flock of sheep and lambs, or jumping into a pond among the ducks and geese; and however loud the old woman might call, or however fast Little Blue Hood might run, he wouldn't come back until he had frightened the whole flock and driven them into a corner, and sent the ducks and geese quacking and gabbling and splashing out of the pond. After his bath he would give himself a good shaking, then begin to dance before his pretty mistress, and saying as well as he could in his barking language, "Isn't it jolly fun? Didn't you see how I made the whole lot scuttle off, and caused that leg of mutton to leave off scratching that sheep's head? I thought a run would do you good, and I did it to make you laugh, for I can't make it out at all, why you have spoken to me so seldom lately? If you don't talk to me oftener, I'll run up to the first bull I see, and try to lay hold of him by the nose, for I would do any thing to hear you speak a little oftener than you do."

And Trot often ran off a great distance, not taking the slightest notice if the old woman called to him, but returning the instant he heard the voice of Little Blue Hood, as if he had said to himself, "That's what I wanted, that's what I ran away to find, and now I found it, I'll go back again;" for the dog acted at times as if he had some such thoughts; and when he went so far, the old woman was compelled to say to the child, "Call the dog back," for fear they should lose him; then Little Blue Hood would send out her sweet silvery voice, and make all the air ring again.

One day, as they sat down on the warm turf of a sloping upland to eat their dinner, the old woman said, "You may talk now as much as you like while we stay here, unless you see some one coming to us."

"Oh! I am so glad," replied Little Blue Hood; "and am sure that I should soon love you, if you would only let me talk to you, and tell you all I think and feel; for I should not be so unhappy, if you would only let me talk to you."

"You could talk about nothing that would at all interest me," answered the old woman; "I'm sure at times the birds make noise enough, and I often wish they were silent. I wonder what they find to make such a noise about?"

"I often fancy, when I am listening to them attentively that I understand what they say to one another," replied Little Blue Hood, giving utterance to what she had imagined at times, while walking in silence beside the old woman. "That one calls to another to come to its nest, and see how clean and pretty its young ones look. That this one has just opened its eyes, and that one has begun to peck, while another is so strong that he has got out of the nest by himself, and is standing on a branch half hidden by the leaves. That another brings food in its pretty beak, and says, ' While you are eating that, I'll sing you a song ;' and I often wish I were a little bird ; then I could talk as much as I liked to my companions among the leaves, instead of being silent for hours together, as I am now. Why do you wish me not to talk ?"

"Because I do not want you to be known, lest you should be taken from me," replied the wicked old woman, though so far speaking the truth. "Because, if I lose you, I have no one to care for me, since my son, your father, is so unkind to me. Because, people believing you to be deaf and dumb, are kinder to you, and also to me, for your sake. If you wish to be taken from me, talk ; tell people who I am, and all I have done ; then you will hear them cry shame on your father, while they pity me. Now, everybody who sees you loves you for being so kind to your poor old grandmother, and for doing your duty to her, as you are doing."

Little Blue Hood thought her very hardest for a few moments, for, although she felt there was something wrong somewhere in what the old woman said, she had never before been called upon to reason against falsehood and cunning, and was for some moments at a loss to know how to reply ; at last she said, "But is it not very wrong to get people to pity us, by saying I am deaf and dumb when I am not ?"

"I do not say you were born so," replied the old woman sharply. "Shall I tell them you are deaf to all they would say against me ; and dumb, because you will not speak, lest by doing so you might injure your poor old grandmother ? How could I make them understand me, if even I said so ?"

Such false reasoning was beyond the reach of the child. She knew what the old woman said was not the truth, but was unable to disentangle the web and get at the falsehood ; for, in her truthful innocence, she carried a light to search for darkness. "I am deaf and dumb," she reasoned to herself, "to do good for grandmother: if I seem to hear and to talk, my voice may be known, and they will take me away ; and that, she says, will make her very unhappy. She is old and poor, and I will stay with her, and do all I can to make her happy ; for that will be doing my duty."

So, listening to the pleading of her good and charitable heart, Little Blue Hood unconsciously wandered along a false path. But an angel trod kindly behind her, and though the track of the pathway she traversed was bordering on the broad way of Error, it still led heavenward, and was hardened by the print of her pretty feet. And there are many narrow Christian paths lying as close to the Waste of Error worn by those who do their duty, and faint not by the way—a sad journey taken by loving hearts —who only meet with their reward when they reach the end, and who never turn back for either praise or blame.

> "For a spirit pure as hers,
> Is pure even while it errs.
> As sunshine glancing on a rill,
> Though turned aside, is sunshine still."
>   T. MOORE.

CHAPTER XIII.

THE LOST CLUE.

LITTLE Blue Hood and her dog had many times gone
through their performance before those who were sent
out in search of her, without their suspecting, for a moment,
that they had but to put out their arms and seize the treas-
ure they so eagerly sought. No doubt the fearlessness of
the old woman prevented suspicion, as she sought the
most public thoroughfares, and if there was a crowd, en-
deavored to pass through the midst of it.

Only once was she stopped by a keen-eyed Detective,
and asked if she had performed before such a mansion,
meaning that where the child last saw her mother; when
she replied that she had and named the day and hour,
hoping, as she said, they wished to see her perform again,
and telling him how generously they had rewarded her.

The only one who discovered that Little Blue Hood was
not dark, was an illiterate countryman, who could neither
read nor write, and knew nothing about the reward offered
for her; though it was posted up at the bar of the village
alehouse, he was too fond of frequenting. "See that,
Jack," he said, pointing to a small rent in the child's stock-
ing, "she's got as white a skin as your little Sall." His
companion saw it, and thought no more about the matter.
The old woman's sharp eyes also saw in a moment what
they had discovered, and was careful in preventing such
mishaps afterwards.

From no quarter could any clue be obtained that was

likely to lead to the recovery of Little Blue Hood. Only
one man was found who had taken particular notice of
her and the old woman, on the day she was stolen. This
was a bricklayer's laborer, who was coming out of a
narrow passage, with a ladder on his shoulder, with which
he was very near running against the child. He had drawn
back, and waited until they passed, and what made him
notice them more particularly, was the courtesy the little
girl made him for drawing back.

Even his description of the dog was correct; but on the
day he gave his evidence to a Detective, who promised to
call on him again in the evening, the ladder he was mount-
ing with a hod full of bricks broke from under him, when
he fell on his head, and had ever since been in the hospital,
and unable to answer a question; and there was but little
hope of his ever recovering.

The parents of Little Blue Hood had, more than once,
driven up to the hospital to inquire how the poor patient
was getting on; they had also seen the head physician,
who had promised to do all that could be done towards
his recovery: but he still remained unconscious, and had
nothing happened he could have told but little more than
he made known to the police officer. The carriage was
afterwards driven to the very spot where the poor man
had seen the old woman and child; and the heart of the
fond mother sank within her, as she glanced at the neighborhood which her child had been brought into.

"Better a thousand times," she said to her husband,
bursting into tears, "that she were dead, and that I knew
where she was laid; for that would be some solace to me,
only to know that the day would come when I should
lie down and sleep my long sleep beside her. But oh! to

think that she may be concealed in some of these crowded
courts and unhealthy alleys, where vice seems to have
made its home ; where she can hear nothing that is good,
and only be taught what is evil: these thoughts are worse
than death, for then I should know that she was at rest,
and look with hope towards that eternal home beyond the
grave, where we shall at last meet never again to part.''

"Hope is a great comforter," replied her husband ;
"and whatever the woman may be she was here seen
with, I have such faith in the innocent and winning ways
of our dear child, as to believe that no one, unless utterly
dead to all that forms the true nature of woman, will ever
treat her unkindly.   Heaven ordains all things for our
good ; and, whatever the ordeal may be that she has to
pass through, it is my faith that she will come out of it
spotless and purified, and that we shall be spared to bless
the day that doomed her to these trials."   His voice trem-
bled, and his lip quivered as he spoke, telling that he felt
her loss as much as his lady did, although he shed no
tears.

Little did they think that their darling was then trailing
with weary feet along the brown, barren highways of
Surrey, compelled to remain silent through the cunning
of a selfish old woman, who trusted to the affectionate
nature of the child, and her sense of duty, for retaining
the strong hold she already had of her.   True, there were
moments when that lady thought, that if ever it should be
the will of Providence to restore her child, she would be
changed into some poor ragged outcast, who had herded
with the very poor, picked up much of their language and
habits, and so unlike the dear Little Blue Hood she had
lost, that she almost dreaded to think what her feelings

would be if she ever met with her after such a change had taken place. Then she prayed to be delivered from such thoughts, and better feelings came; in which her heart told her that, whatever the condition of the child might be, she would be dearer to her through having suffered; that however beautiful her flower might have been at its opening, she could not hope it would escape all the bitter blasts to which it must be exposed—transplanted to such a neighborhood as she had visited—uninjured.

Money had been scattered with a free hand, in every direction, where there seemed to be the remotest chance of recovering the lost child ; but all was useless ;—for, while those who were paid were searching for her in the great network of streets and squares, courts and alleys, that make up wide-spreading London, she was walking forth in the open noon of day on the highways that stretch out among the suburbs.

Many an eye had looked on the performance of Little Blue Hood that would have brightened with joy, and sought no other reward than the happiness of restoring her to her parents. Who, under that dark-stained skin would look for the little mole on her pretty shoulder, which, in her playful moods, her dear mother, while kissing and fondling her, had often called a little strawberry, and pretended to want to bite it off; while Little Blue Hood had screamed with delight and laughter, as she laid her sweet face on her mother's neck, overhung by her long silky tresses ?

And often the child thought of all that love, and all that fond play, and all those warm tender kisses, which were showered on her every hour of the day, as she dragged her weary feet along the dusty roads, with Trot sticking close to her side, and often looked up strangely at her sad face, as if he too remembered the happy days they had passed together.

And that voice! No argument used by her husband, or her friends, was able to convince her that she had not heard her daughter call to her, when the carriage slackened its pace, beside the little wood. The Detective called —had an interview with her—described the old woman and child; giving also a minute description of the dog, and offering to produce all three any day her Ladyship might be pleased to appoint.

No; she did not for a moment believe that the little dark dancing girl was her daughter; that thought she had entirely dismissed from her mind. But the voice! No power upon earth could convince her that she had not heard her daughter call to her. And there were times when she thought that voice was still sounding in her ears as it went winging its way to heaven, and that at the time she fancied she heard it, her child was dying—for grief leaves strange impressions on the mind, and the cry of "mother," in that out-of-the-way place, was one of those mysteries which none of her friends could unravel.

CHAPTER XIV.

THE HOVEL.

MANY long weeks had by this time passed away, and the green of Summer had faded into the solemn gold of Autumn, when the old woman and Little Blue Hood were on their way back to London, having only twice visited the old house in the Borough since the day the child saw her mother in the carriage.

The old woman was the first to suffer from the fatigue to which she had so long exposed the child, while Little Blue Hood seemed to grow stronger every day ; for the fresh air and the sweet sunshine fell like blessings upon her, and she was much healthier than she ever would have been had she remained with her dear mother.

There was no need to stain her pretty face and neck now, so tawny had the summer sun made her, that she was as brown as a little gypsy. She could walk more miles a day than the old woman, and was at times quite happy and light-hearted, as she was now allowed to talk whenever she pleased, excepting in the presence of stran‧ gers.

As for Trot, he had grown quite fat, and was almost too lazy to dance : two or three steps on his hinder legs were all he could be persuaded to do, when down he went on all fours again, for almost everybody they came near had fed him ; and, on more than one occasion, his little mis‧ tress had been compelled to lay him on his back and roll him, for fear he should burst his skin ; for the little glut‧ ton had eaten till it was quite tight.

As for the old woman, the avenger seemed now to be treading hard on her heels, as if demanding retribution for the injury she had inflicted on that mother and child. She now suffered through a deep cough, which made her shake in her old shoes every time it came on, and pre-vented her from walking again until it was over. And, often after it had passed away, she was compelled to sit down anywhere until she recovered.

It made the tender heart of Little Blue Hood ache again,

to see her in so much pain ; and she would sit beside her —take hold of her hand, looking pitifully into her old, hard, cruel, wrinkled face—while inquiring if she felt better.

It had been raining hard for above an hour, when one evening the old woman's fit of coughing was worse than it had ever been before, and she sank down by the roadside, saying that she could walk no further, though it was above two miles to the cottage where she had made arrangements to lodge for the night, having stayed there before several times.

The rain increased, and the evening shadows began to deepen, and even the Autumn noise of brooks in the neighboring wood became hushed ; but the old woman was unable to walk more than a few yards, leaning her hand heavily on the willing shoulder of the child ; and there was no house nearer than the roadside cottage, where they intended to sleep.

Faster came down the rain, which the wind, now blowing a gale, beat into their faces, and the trees roared again as they lashed their branches together, while the gray leaden-colored sky hung so low that it seemed to touch the topmost boughs of the trees.

"Let me lie down and die here," said the old woman, sitting on the bank by the woodside. "I can walk no further. Oh, what a lonely place this is to die in !"

It was indeed lonesome, and was seldom traversed excepting on a market day, when the villagers went to the little town which the old woman and child had left that morning ; for being a branch road, there was scarcely any traffic on it at any other time.

"Oh ! what shall we do ?" exclaimed Little Blue Hood,

clasping her hands together, and never thinking of herself, although she was wet to the skin. "If, after you have rested a bit, you could walk a little further, only to the next field where that white gate is, there is such a nice shed there, where we saw the pretty calves, and you laid down and went to sleep on the clean straw when it was so hot. Oh! do try to pray for God to send one of His angels to help you to walk, for it is but a little way, and I always found He sent an angel to help me when I was in trouble and prayed to Him."

"I will try," said the old woman, rising with difficulty and walking in great pain. "But do not ask me to pray; I don't know how. I am too wicked to pray. Rest, rest is all I need; lead me on and let me lie down."

Although not more than a hundred yards off, they were a long time reaching the gate, which was easily undone, as it was only fastened by a staple, hasp, and iron pin; and as there were only a cow and her calf inside, with plenty of dry litter, a bed, such as it was, was soon made up in one corner of the cowshed, and on it the old woman lay down. A few weeks earlier, and the hovel would not have afforded them such comfort; for it was fortunately that turning of the season, when the fields, though yielding but scanty pasturage, are not bare enough to require cattle to be driven into the strawyard, but with a little fodder placed in the shed at night, allows them to remain out in the daytime, to pick up what little remains of the after-math of grass. The cow was a quiet meek-eyed animal, and allowed herself to be moved out of her warm place, without showing the least sign of anger; while the calf began licking the hand of Little Blue Hood as she stroked its head, as if it knew that she would do it no

harm. Trot rolled himself up into the smallest possible
space in the far corner, as if he knew that the best thing
he could do under all circumstances was to get out of the
way, and go to sleep as soon as he could. Sometimes he
raised his old-fashioned head above the straw, when he
heard the old woman moaning in her pain, but it was down
again in an instant, as if he said to himself, "Oh! it's
only her; I don't care for her; I was afraid it was my
little mistress."

"I am so cold," said the old woman in a faint voice,
what few teeth she had left, chattering again in her old
gums, "that I feel as if I should die unless I have something to warm me. Feel in the large cloak pocket, and
you'll find——." But she was too exhausted to say any
more, and again sank with her head on the straw which
the child had also heaped plentifully over her. She ex-
amined the large cloak pocket, and found a little wicker-
covered flask of brandy, a box of matches, some tea and
sugar screwed up in separate papers, beside other things.
She then opened the little basket in which the old woman
carried their provisions, and took out a tin can which
they often used for milk, getting it warm as it came from
the cow, when they found anybody milking in the fields.
Little Blue Hood had seen the old woman light a fire, and
boil water in the can, and finding a couple of loose bricks,
she placed them edgeways near the door, where she cleared a space of ground, removing every morsel of litter that
was likely to catch fire and spread over the shed ; and
this done she pulled to pieces an old dry worn-out birch
besom, which had been thrown into a corner, and soon
kindled a fire under the can, having filled it with water
from a tub that stood outside the shed. When the water

boiled she put in some tea, which she let stand over the fire for a few minutes, and then carefully took out every leaf with the spoon, and having put in some sugar and a little brandy, she made a tray of an old milk-can lid which she found on the floor, and then took the refreshing beverage to the old woman, who sat up, and as it was so hot, sipped it with the spoon as well as she could.

The kindness of Little Blue Hood pierced the old woman's heart deeper than any thing before had ever done, for she felt that she must have died—as the cold was gradually creeping all over her—had it not been for the child ; and her guilty conscience stung her, like a serpent, when her little benefactress took up the spoon and gave her the drink, for her withered hand shook so, she could not help herself without spilling it, after she had taken the first two or three spoonfuls.

"Oh! I am unworthy of this kindness," said the old woman, again lying down ; "and it is more pain to me to receive it from your hands than the pangs I otherwise suffer. If you knew all, you would hate me, and wish I were dead—dead."

"I could never have so wicked a thought," said Little Blue Hood, "as to wish my grandmother dead"—the old woman groaned again—"and if my being so near to you makes you feel unhappy, I will go into the corner with Trot, where it is growing dark, and wait there without speaking a word, until you call me. I will do any thing I can to help to make you better. Do not say it pains you to see me do things for you; I am but a little girl, and shall know how to attend on you better than I do now, when I grow bigger."

"It is not that. You cannot know what it is that pains me so," said the old woman grasping the straw in her

5

hands, as she writhed under an accusing conscience. "No one can do things better than you; nobody was ever so kind to me before as you are, and bore so long with me with patience. I do not know what I should do without you now. Now make yourself some tea, and dry your little feet; then come and lie down beside me: I am warm now, and feel a little better, and think I can sleep."

Little Blue Hood did as the old woman bade her; moving about almost as noiselessly as a shadow, for fear of disturbing the old woman, and only putting a bit or two of stick on the fire at a time, lest the crackling of the fuel might awake her. There was plenty of provisions in the basket, and Trot, well knowing what was going on, soon came out of his hiding-place, and began to beg; and after she had fed her dog, and had her tea, and dried her feet, and given another cupful to the old woman, she knelt down upon the straw to say her prayers.

With clasped hands and upraised face, she closed her pretty blue eyes, and prayed to the Lord to make the old woman better, and cause her to pray also. Prayed that she might do her duty, and think of doing good to others, more than of herself. And Trot sat motionless beside her, and never stirred until she arose from kneeling, when he jumped under the straw, and laid down beside her, coiling himself up under her arm. Night darkened over the lowly cowshed, which the breath of the cattle made warm; and excepting having to get up once or twice to attend on the old woman, Little Blue Hood rested as quietly, and slept as soundly as if she had lain on a bed of the softest down.

CHAPTER XV.

THE COTTAGE.

THOUGH the old woman was too weak, on the following morning, to walk so far as the pretty little roadside cottage, at which they had beforetime lodged, she, after much persuasion, allowed the child to go by herself, and get Nanny to hire any kind of a conveyance that could be got from the neighboring village, to carry her from the hovel.

Nanny, the owner of the cottage, was a clean little old woman, with hair of that yellowish white that looks so much like raw silk, instead of the silvery-gray oftener seen. Her cottage, which was her own little freehold, stood by itself, and was full a quarter of a mile from the village, and, excepting when she happened to have lodgers, she lived there all alone, as she had done for above forty long years.

Little Blue Hood liked old Nanny and her cottage better than anybody, or any place she had stayed at since she was stolen from her own dear home; for she had been allowed to say what she liked, and do what she pleased, while there.

It was a beautiful morning after the rain, and the child quite enjoyed the walk, with Trot barking and bounding beside her, and would have been very happy but for the thought of the old woman being so ill. The cottage was buried in trees, and covered with ivy, which reached to the very tops of the chimneys; while on the thatched roof grew stone-crop, and no end of moss and lichen—green, golden, and gray: and when the sun shone be tween the stems of the trees on the clean windows, making them glitter like gold, and throwing a network of shadows on the floor from the overhanging sprays, it looked one of the prettiest places the eye ever dwelt upon, excepting in a picture.

The old woman was in her garden tying up the chrysanthemums and dahlias, which the wind and rain overnight had beaten down, and no sooner did she hear the sound of approaching footsteps, than she raised herself from her stooping position, and, looking over the low hedge through her spectacles, she said, "Heart alive! I thought I knew the sound of thy little footsteps; and why didn't you come last night? and where is your grandmother?"

The child told her how she had left the old woman ill in the cowshed, where they had passed the night, and that she was to go to the village and get some kind of conveyance to bring her to the cottage, and was not to mind the expense.

"Poor old woman! pretty dear child! come inside, and let me make you a nice breakfast, while I go and get William, the old carrier, to come with his cart. It is one of his off-days; if it wasn't, I don't know where I could get a conveyance for her either for love or money; unless it was Farmer Clay's great wagon, and his four fat horses. Sleeping in a cowshed! and such a night as it was. She may well be ill: and I wonder both of you haven't caught your deaths of cold."

But Little Blue Hood would neither stay to have her breakfast, nor wait to ride back in the old carrier's cart, as she knew the old woman was too ill to be left alone; so having delivered her message, and made Nanny understand where the hovel was, she hurried back, saying, "I shall be standing at the gate, watching for him, and he will be sure to see me."

Trot, however, had a good breakfast of bread and milk, before he went back; beside a plate of scraps, which Nanny had saved up for him; and he didn't seem at all in any hurry to leave after having finished his meal.

Old Nanny never did things by halves; for, when the carrier stopped before her cottage with his cart, she placed an old coverlet on the bottom, laying on it one of her beds, with a pillow ; and, as she said, "Every thing to make the old grandmother comfortable ;" and, when all was done, she locked her door, and rode with him in the cart. It was well she went ; for the old woman was so stiff in her joints, that she was unable to walk, and thankful she was when she reached Nanny's cottage, and was put into her nice clean bed ; for the old woman liked cleanliness.

And there Little Blue Hood nursed her, running up and down stairs a hundred times a day, to fetch and carry away every thing she wanted, and never seeming to think that she had done enough.

And now a strange change came over the old woman, and she seemed to feel as if her very life depended on her retaining the child. It was no longer the sordid feeling of keeping her because of the money she brought in by her dancing, but a consciousness that, in all her long life, she had never met with anybody who had shown for her such affection, served her so faithfully, and studied her every wish.

That she had in every instance returned good for evil,

never betrayed her by word or deed, and now that she was ill and helpless, attended to her every want, and administered to her with so gentle a hand, that there were times when—had she been strong enough—she could have got out of bed, thrown herself at the feet of Little Blue Hood, and while she knelt, asking for forgiveness, told her all she had done. But her wicked and selfish nature still reigned uppermost, and when she resolved at times to tell her all—to confess that she was in no way related to her, that she had carried her away from her dear mother and her happy home, to feed an imaginary vengeance—not but what she believed the child's father had injured her—the fear of losing her forever prevailed over these weak resolutions, and made her feel that without Little Blue Hood, her life would be miserable.

Strong in her love as in her hatred, she now, instead of using threats, as she had done at first to retain her, showed her the greatest affection that a heart so selfish as hers was capable of entertaining for any thing, excepting herself. But, amid all this fondness for the child, she never once thought of restoring her to her parents; neither did Little Blue Hood, while the old woman was so ill, ever express a wish to return to her dear mother, though her little heart often yearned towards home; for, she said to herself, "It would be wicked to wish to leave her now she is so ill; and though Nanny is very kind, she likes nobody to wait on her but me. Oh, how I wish dear mother was here to help to make her well, then take her home with us."

Strange, that instead of looking at the injury she had inflicted on the child and her parents, and feeling only the deepest remorse for what she had done; she tried to find consolation in the thought that she had never starved or beaten her, and that, however she might have disliked her at first, she now loved her; and she mistook this selfish fondness for the child for repentance. But, stranger than all, she now liked to hear the dear child say her prayers; and often asked her to pray for her, that she might be forgiven.

And, in her simple way, Little Blue Hood offered up her prayers from lips as pure, and a heart as innocent, as ever supplicated the Throne of Mercy for forgiveness. The old woman also became so resigned at last, that she could bear to hear the child pray to God to bless and protect her dear mother and father, without groaning, as she did at first, when, with folded hands, and closed eyes, Little Blue Hood knelt beside her.

Her wicked hard heart was touched at last, although it was but slightly; for, as the slow-falling drop at length wears away granite, so had the unceasing kindness of the child worn away every feeling of dislike the old woman once had towards her.

"I do not know how it is," said the old woman, "but when you are praying, or reading out of that Holy Book, which I scarcely ever looked into during all the years I have lived, the evil faces that sometimes haunt me seem afraid, and go away; and while I can keep all wicked thoughts from my mind, and pray to myself to be forgiven, all the wrong I have done, there are moments when I seem to feel happier than ever I have felt so far back as I can remember."

"I have often heard the good clergyman that used to visit my dear mother, and take me on his knee and teach me to read, say, 'that prayer was the bridge that spanned from earth to heaven;' and when I have looked at the rainbow, have thought what a beautiful bridge it would be to walk over, and to see the angels waiting to receive me on the other side ; and then, to hear the music of heaven sounding, and to walk, holding my mother's hand, in a land of flowers, where it is always summer, and no night ever comes to make the blossoms shut up."

The child raised her dear blue eyes as she ceased speaking, and, as the sunshine fell around her, it threw streaks of gold upon her hair which, here and there, showed portions of its rich natural color through the dye, that was slowly wearing off.

"You are pure and innocent, and have no sin weighing you down like a mountain," said the old woman, clasping her wrinkled hands, and moving them up and down, as she closed her eyes ; "while I—while I—" Then tears checked her utterance ; they were the first she had shed for her sins. The rock was smitten at last, by an Invisible hand, and though the stream that trickled out was very feeble, it was a Healing Water that flowed. She then added, "I can never hope to be forgiven for the injury I have done to you and yours, and which you will know all about one day, before I die."

"Whatever it may be," replied Little Blue Hood, "it will be as nothing to what Our Saviour suffered to save such as you and me. They scourged Him, and nailed Him to the cruel cross, yet He forgave them what they did."

"That is true, for it is written in the Holy Book," said the old woman, as if speaking to herself. "But

I? what have I not done? To me, until now, revenge ever seemed sweeter than forgiveness. It is you that have taught me to forgive. To return injury for injury, and too often evil for good, was the feeling that sprung up, like rank weeds, from my sinful nature. In my blindness, I called revenge justice, and believed that wrong for wrong was fulfilling a right law; for I had seen that law demand life for life, and stood under the gallows until it had gorged its fill, and was satisfied. But I feel that while you remain with me, I can never be what I once was any more."

Then the old woman would fall asleep, and sometimes while she slept, her lips would move, as if in prayer. At others, she would awake with a sudden start, and a cry ringing in her ears of "My child! my child!" seeming to be the same voice that she heard beside the wood, shrieking for Little Blue Hood, while she was dragging her through the sharp thorns and briers of the entangled underwood. Then she would pray again to be forgiven, though her conscience told her all the while, that the true work of repentance would never begin aright, until she restored that dear child to her sorrowful parents. Then she deceived herself, by trying to believe that Little Blue Hood had been sent to her by an All-wise Providence, to make her repent of her evil ways; and so tried to stifle "the still small voice."

CHAPTER XVI.

THE STREET-HAWKERS.

THE fresh air that blew through every window of the cottage, the kind attention of Nanny in preparing every thing that she thought would do her good, and, above all, the incessant attention and careful nursing of Little Blue Hood, soon restored the old woman, though she never again enjoyed her usual health.

True to her old habits, she no sooner found herself well enough, than she pined to return to her native London air; for the child had given her solemn promise that she would never leave her until she wished her to do so, and she knew that Little Blue Hood would sooner die than utter a wilful falsehood. "I like to see the shop-windows, and to walk through the crowded streets, and hear the hum and noise of the people," said the old woman to Nanny; "the very stillness that you are so fond of, and that no noise ever breaks, would soon be the death of me, though the child seems as fond of it as you are."

"Bring her to stay a month or two with me next summer," said Nanny, kissing the dear child before they departed; "it shall cost you nothing; and remember, if any thing is likely to happen to yourself, send for me, and I'll set off the very hour I receive your letter; and if you wish it, the pretty darling shall have a home with me as long as I live; and when it pleases God to call me away, I'll leave it to her, and a little something else beside." And she dried her tears on her apron, after she had unclasped her arms from the child's neck.

The old woman made a kind of half promise, which she
hardly wished to fulfil ; for she was jealous of the affection Nanny showed for Little Blue Hood. When she
reached the old Borough, she had her goods removed to
the house of the little widow, who had been her servant
in former years, and up to the time Edith's father threw
up his brief, and refused to proceed with her trial. The
poor woman had lost her husband, and was left with a
large family ; the eldest of which had lived for a little time
with the old woman, as we have before stated, and was
much older, though not much bigger, than Little Blue
Hood. But this shrewd child was as thorough a little
woman at going to market and driving a hard bargain, as
her clean, industrious little mother, who went out charing
and washing, and left the house and the children to the
care of this experienced and old-fashioned little girl.

"Peggy," said the old woman to the little widow when
she took the apartment, "we always did agree together,
and I hope we always shall ; you knew me in better days,
and were always a good and faithful servant. I am not
what I was. I have reason for keeping my own secret,
and know how sinful it is to tell a falsehood. Ask me no
questions about this dear child ; you shall know all some
day. And do not question her yourself."

The little widow, who was truth itself, promised her
old mistress that she would neither question her, nor the
child, and so it was settled, and they entered their apartment in one of the noisiest but cleanest courts of the old
Borough.

Although the old woman never undeceived the child by
telling her that she was not her grandmother, she told her
that she was poor, and did not conceal that her dancing

had produced a deal of money; but that in future, she did not intend to endeavor to obtain a livelihood by such means, but to go about selling things, which would be a more reputable pursuit, and afford profit enough to support them.

"Oh, we will sell flowers, grandmother," said Little Blue Hood; "I should so like that; then I shall be a little flower-girl, and all the ladies and gentlemen will buy my pretty flowers."

"But there are no flowers in winter that we could afford to buy, and sell cheap," replied the old woman; "in spring and summer they will be plentiful. There are other things that we can go around with, that please children, and have a ready sale, such as dolls, shell baskets, little purses, and pretty boxes, pincushions, and toys, such as children are always breaking, and their mothers replacing. They will be light to carry, and every shilling we take will leave sixpence profit. Though a poor, we shall get an honest living; and I do not care what I do to see you happy, and keep us together."

With all her cunning, the old woman could not get Little Blue Hood to promise that, if she saw her mother, she would not go to her. With that exception, the child said she would not attempt to escape from her; and in her own mind she felt certain that, if she chanced to meet with her mother, she would take them both home, and that the old woman would live in the apartments which were always called grandmother's; for it was true enough that her father's mother was living abroad in a warm climate for the benefit of her health. Little Blue Hood believed that the old woman was the same grandmother who went away when she herself was but a little baby, and had no remembrance of her; and that through some unkindness of her father's, she objected to return.

With all her love for the child, the old woman felt that she could not restore her; that were she to leave her, her life would be miserable; so she determined to restrict their rounds to such neighborhoods as her mother was never likely to visit, and that was one reason why she stocked her basket with such homely wares.

Among the many lessons impressed on the mind of Little Blue Hood, by her fond and pious mother, not one was more duly enforced than that of being kind to, and respecting the poor. She was shown that all labor, however humble the calling, was respectable; that nothing was more disgraceful than idleness, which was the root of many evils, and that those poor little girls and boys, who toiled and wearied themselves in the streets in their endeavors to obtain an honest livelihood, did more good in the world than many who were heirs of wealth, and who never either toiled or spun; but that those poor children, by their exertions, supplied things that others wanted, and, by such means, provided for wants of their own.

These lessons were never forgotten by that dutiful and intelligent child, and they helped to root out every feeling of improper pride from her heart: for there is a pride—that of excelling in doing well—which is not improper, and which never ought to be destroyed, though narrow-minded people persist in calling it ambition. Such a pride increases instead of lessening our respect towards the possessor; if applause only is not sought to be won by it; for then it verges into vanity.

Little Blue Hood was too young and simple and innocent, to know what is meant by filling a high station in life, and having been taught that there was no disgrace in honest labor, she sallied out with her little basket of cheap ware on her arm, and felt as proud of it as if she had been going to scatter flowers in the pathway of a queen.

Beside her walked the old woman—who now stooped in her gait—with one hand resting on the child's shoulder, and had they caught a poet's eye, he would have likened Little Blue Hood to Spring leading along aged Winter. She timed her light elastic step to the slow pace of the now feeble old woman, as they moved slowly from street to street, only offering their ware to such as stopped them, and inquired the price of the articles they wanted to purchase.

It was a life that suited Trot to a T; he had again the run of the streets, could fight any dog he had a mind to pick a quarrel with, and, if he were likely to have the worst of it, run to his pretty mistress for safety, who was sure to take him up and carry him, until he was out of danger. Then, he passed such a lot of butchers' shops during the day, and as the doors were always open, it was as easy to run in and out again, as it was to gallop along the streets ; and if there happened to be any thing handy that took his fancy, he was sure to have it.

How an old woman stared one day, as she dropped her mutton chop, while feeling for the halfpence to pay for it. She thought there must have been a hole somewhere in the shop-floor, and began feeling about among the sawdust to find it ; while Trot, making but one mouthful of it, had, after a few shakes of his head to help it down, swallowed it bone and all.

One day, a Punch-and-Judy-man, who was toiling alone,

carrying his tall cumbrous show on his back, looked hard at Trot, and pointing him out to his companion, said, "If he wasn't all black, I could take my 'happy David,' that that ere dog was our old Bob, wot we lost one day at the West-end."

Trot knew his old master well enough, and had not forgotten the many beatings he received from his hands when he was first made to dance, so set off home as fast as his legs would carry him ; as he often did when he was pursued for thieving, or had stolen any thing that was too big to be eaten at one meal in the street, such as a bullock's heart, or the piece of round of beef they were cutting cheap steaks off from the block. More than once Little Blue Hood had to pay for his robberies.

What numbers of poor people bought the cheap articles Little Blue Hood sold, only because she was so pretty and gentle, and had such a low sweet voice, and was so kind to the old woman she led about ; getting her to sit down when she was tired, and taking such care of her. And the old woman was never weary of talking of her kindness, and telling the people how good she was ; until poor mothers pointed her out to their children, whenever she passed, as an example to be followed.

Then they began to ask her for things that she had not got at first, such as cotton and thread, pins and needles, tapes, buttons, and such like articles, as the very poor are ever needing ; and these the old woman soon procured ; and, by the time winter was over, and there was a cry of "Come, buy my pretty primroses," in the streets of the mouldy old Borough, Little Blue Hood had got quite a connection around the neighborhood, and had only to call on her regular customers as she went her rounds ; doing her business, though on a very small scale, on the same principle as many of the largest commercial houses, who send out their daily travellers, to receive orders and deliver goods. The profit was cent. per cent. on many of these trifling articles, and poor as many of her customers were, they would say, "God bless the pretty child ! never mind the farthing change."

In fact, Little Blue Hood and the old woman did, in their way, what is called "a roaring trade."

CHAPTER XVII.

THE LITTLE COURT.

LIKE a sudden burst of sweet sunshine in a sad and shady place, such a light did the presence of Little Blue Hood shed on that narrow and high-walled court in the Borough. Those, whose nature was as coarse as their clothes, always spoke kindly to her, or smiled and nodded whenever she passed their doors. There was not a dirty or ragged child in the place, but what was ready to run as far as its little bare feet would carry it to serve her. If only her shoes were soiled, they were ready to fight for the privilege of kneeling down, and rubbing off the dirt with their tattered jacket cuffs. They would wait about the entrance of the court to be allowed to carry her basket a little way for her when she set out of a morning, and watch at the corners of all the streets in the neigh-

borhood for her return in the evening : and right proud
was the little fellow who happened to hit on the right
street, when he came bearing her basket in triumph up
the court. Let them but see her and the old woman waiting to cross the road, and at the risk of their lives, they
would dash over amongst the horses and hurrying vehicles, one carrying Trot, who was on friendly terms with
them all ; another, the basket ; while a third and fourth
led the child and old woman safely and gently across.
They would fight to pump for her, and never think they
had washed out the jug often enough, if they knew the
water was wanted for Little Blue Hood.

The little widow's noisy and uproarious children were
like lambs under the eye of Little Blue Hood. Jack
would wash his dirty face and hands at her bidding, if she
would promise to comb his hair afterwards, while, had
his mother commanded him, he would very likely have
said, "I shan't for you ;" then he would have got his
jacket dusted with a cane, and roared again until he raised
the whole court.

There was something so gentle in her voice, and so winning in her sweet face, that only to look at her made all
the children love her. If they were making use of naugh-
ty language, and only saw her, their lips were sealed in a
moment ; and nothing delighted them so much as to get
her seated on a stool, while they sat round her on the flag-
ged pavement of the court, in the mild spring evenings,
and joined their voices in the pretty songs and hymns she
taught them to sing ; or read to them some amusing story,
which the old woman had bought for her.

Then she would invent some new game, in which Trot
could join ; and, what with the barking of the dog, the

6

laughing, shouting, clapping of hands, and pattering of little feet, as they tried to catch her and Trot, that court was the merriest, happiest, noisiest little place to be found in the whole Borough. Sometimes she would bring out her tambourine, and make Trot dance with her for their amusement.

"Bless her dear heart," said Peggy, speaking to a neighbor, as she was going out to a hard day's washing, in a damp, dark, underground kitchen, which was worse than the thickest November fog, when filled with the steam from the copper; "I'm sure mine are hardly like the same children since she came to live with us. The lads never swear now, nor threaten to knock their sisters' heads off; but kneel down, and say their 'Our Father' to her of a night, and their 'Grace before Meat;' and they don't get the treacle-pot, and rub one another's faces with it; nor mix the salt with the sugar, to make a pudding; nor clean the window with the candle-end, then rub it on the looking-glass; nor catch flies, and put them into little Sally's mouth, as they used to; nor swim my shoes in the wash-tub; nor put the ashes in the tea-kettle. I never saw such a change in my born days, as there is in 'em. Then she makes them as clean as new pins, and takes them to church with her on a Sunday; and they seem so pleased when she comes back, and tell me how good they all 'was,' that I can't help sitting down sometimes and having a good cry to myself, when I think that such a dear little thing, as she is, should make us all so happy."

Sometimes Little Blue Hood went out with the eldest daughter a marketing, and saw how she bantered the butcher down, as she bargained for a lot of trimmings, which had been cut off to make the joints look fresh and

neat; also offering a penny for a rasher of bacon they
asked three halfpence for, peeping at the scales to see that
the grocer gave her good weight, and seizing upon the
largest herring in a moment, if they were all one price.
And this little woman-in-mind, knew where the cheapest
and best bread was sold, and where she could get three
pounds of potatoes for a halfpenny less than at any other
shop; and sometimes she brought home a penny cabbage,
so big, that the largest saucepan they had only held half
of it. And the butcher boys with their greasy hair, the
fishmonger boys with their sticky hands, and the coal-
shed boys with their grimy faces, were all eager to carry
these cheap bargains home when Little Blue Hood accom-
panied Peggy's daughter; for they liked to walk beside
her, and hear her talk to them, and said among themselves, "She's a real good-un, and no mistake." Let any
strange boy offer her the slightest insult, and every little
jacket in the neighborhood was off, and little dirty fists
knuckled up to "give him pepper."

And Little Blue Hood would listen attentively while
Peggy told her all she had to do in the house, while her
mother went out to work, and what trouble she used to
have to get the children to bed when she was late, until
Edith came to live with them. How baby—as the young-
est was always called—cried when she washed her; and
how, when she gave Jacky the poker to knock it on the
floor while he nursed baby while she cleaned up the
hearth, he sometimes hit it in the face with the poker-nob
and so made baby cry worse. How Sally got all her
dusters to make dolls of; and Billy was fond of getting to
the potatoes, and cutting them into the shapes of boats and
little carts.

"I'm sure they used to nearly drive me mad at times before you came," said little Peggy, using the very words she had heard her mother utter on such occasions.

Let her industrious mother come home at what hour she might, she never went to bed, until she had what she called "given the things a good rummaging, so as to make room for more dirt;" and as Little Blue Hood lay in bed, she could hear her going to the tap and rattling the heavy pail about; and when she got up in the morning, she found the house as clean as if there had never been any children in it to make the least dirt. Little Peggy took after her mother for cleanliness, and was sousing her brothers and sisters all day long, rubbing the soap-suds into their eyes until they cried, then giving them sugar, to keep them quiet, while she dried their well-scrubbed faces.

It amused Little Blue Hood, morning and evening, to see that woman-like child manage her mother's household, when she returned, after going her daily rounds. And many a little sock did that pretty child help to darn, and many a patch did she put on frock or pinafore, which young Peggy could not find time to mend; and in her after days, Little Blue Hood never regretted the lessons she had learned, while living amongst the poor in that little court in the Borough.

CHAPTER XVIII.

THE EAST WIND.

EVERY day saw the old woman grow weaker, and stoop lower, and bear heavier on her stick and the shoulder of Little Blue Hood, as she went out with her; her feet creeping along the ground, for she could no longer lift them up, as she had done beforetime.

The storm of wind and rain that drove her for shelter into the hovel, had left behind a cold that had penetrated her old bones, and made her feel every change of the weather; nor had she ever got rid of the cough, which shook her at times like a galvanic battery.

At last, a bitter east wind set in, and the rheumatism seized upon her tottering limbs, and she was wholly unable to move about at all. Then the old woman knew that her days were drawing to a close, and that the evening shadows would soon darken around her, and she should never again see the light of the sun, "no more forever."

The child tried to persuade her to leave the Borough, and go to Nanny's pretty cottage, where there was plenty of fresh air, and she would be very quiet; but the old woman said, "No; I should like to die here, and be carried to my last resting-place over the stones which my old feet have helped to wear hollow, in my long and weary pilgrimage. And if I get no better, which I don't believe I ever shall any more in this world, you can bring that good clergyman who noticed you in the church, and took you and Peggy's children into the vestry, where he was so kind to them—you can bring him to pray beside me, if he will be good enough to come to the bedside of such a sinner as I am. For there are things that weigh heavily on my mind, that I could never frame my speech to tell rightly to anybody but one of God's good servants, and to the Almighty Himself, when I pray to Him to forgive me my sins : for I feel, my darling, that He has sent the Angel of Death to me in this east wind, and that I shall never leave this house any more, until I am carried across the threshold. I know you have forgiven me for all I have done amiss, and for deceiving you, and telling you that I was your grandmother ; and God will be as good to me as you have been ; for you first turned me from the evil of my ways, through His grace.''

The east wind would have passed over her harmless enough, had she never stolen Little Blue Hood, and exposed herself so much to the elements, which, instead of injuring, had strengthened and hardened the child ; while storm and rain, and cold and long wearisome journeys, had filled the hollows of her old bones with aches and pains, which Death only could put an end to.

Again Little Blue Hood nursed her, read to her, and in her pretty way knelt with folded hands by her bedside, and prayed for her ; while Trot kept watch on a morsel of carpet at the foot of the bed, and never left the room unless it was to follow his pretty mistress, and then he stole in and out noiselessly. Sometimes he would rear up beside the bed, and holding his head on one side, look at her as if he could have said a good deal, had he been so minded. Then he would return to his resting-place, coil himself up, and lie as still as a sleeping mouse. He never once danced all the time the old woman lay dying.

She would not have a doctor sent for ; for, she said to her landlady, "It's very kind of you, Peggy, and you always were kind ; but a doctor is of no use now, for I know that my end is near. I require no one but our darling to be near me; for, when I have hold of her dear hand, I seem at times as if she were leading me into heaven ; and when I sleep, I have heard her in my dreams pleading with the angels at the gates to let me in, and I feel assured that they will open their golden doors for me, for her sake, and listen to her prayers."

She could not rest if Little Blue Hood was out of her sight, and never seemed so happy as when she held the hand of that dear child within her own, or pressed it to her lips. She had told her every thing, and Edith had forgiven her with all her heart, and solemnly promised 'to remain with her, either until she was better, or the time came when "all tears should be wiped from her eyes, and she should never feel pain any more."

When the old woman lay on her death-bed, reproaching herself for what she had done, Little Blue Hood tried to console her by saying, that but for her, she should never have been acquainted with the patience the poor display under all privations ; and that, above all, it made her happy to know that she, a little child, had been the means, through Providence, of leading her to the foot of the Cross.

When the good clergyman came, the old woman concealed nothing from him : and great was his surprise, when he found her passage to the grave had been smoothed by the hand of a little child, and that she was not afraid to die, such faith had she in the promises read to her out of the Holy Book by Little Blue Hood. A doctor was then called in ; for the clergyman felt it a solemn duty to do all he could to prolong the old woman's life. But the doctor held out no hope—he even named the number of hours she might be expected to live.

How Little Blue Hood sorrowed when she was told that she must soon lose her; she knew from her heart that the old woman loved her, as she had never before loved any human soul. She knew that if parting with her heart's blood, drop by drop, would undo the past, and make up for those tears she had caused her to shed, the old woman would have yielded her life slowly and painfully, however much such suffering might have been prolonged.

She admitted to the clergyman how wrongfully she had acted in stealing the child, but could not be brought to confess that she was sorry for having done so ; "for that," said she, "would be saying I was sorry I ever knew her, when she brought to me more true happiness than it was ever my lot to enjoy before."

In this belief she died, avowing "that the finger of Heaven guided her in what she did, and that she had such faith in the prayers and forgiveness of the child, in her own sincere repentance, in the intercession of Our Saviour, and the unbounded mercy of God, that she had no more fear of Death than she had of falling asleep, with the hand of Little Blue Hood clasped between her own."

The clergyman was not a person to throw a gloomy shadow over her pathway to the grave, after the child had brightened it with the light of eternal Hope.

They are no true Christians who would willingly embitter the last moments of the dying, by holding out threats of the doom that lies beyond the grave, where He only sits as Judge, who knoweth the secrets of all hearts, and seeth in human motives, it may be, something redeeming, which we, in our blindness, were never permitted to behold.

When the clergyman proposed that the parents of the child should be sent for, and Little Blue Hood assured the dying woman that she knew, through her interceding, they would forgive her, she shook her head, and said, "No; to see the lady I have caused so much sorrow, would be more than I could endure. I hope to meet her and my darling in heaven, and when there my transgressions will be blotted out, and my sins be remembered no more."

It was the last night, and Little Blue Hood and the old woman were alone; she lay, as usual, very quiet, holding the child's hand; at length she said, in a voice that was audible enough to Edith's attentive ear, though, had another person been in the room, not a word she uttered would have been heard, for the child, through long watching, understood her if she only moved her lips: "I have a last request to make of you, my darling, and I know you will grant it. For it is what you yourself can do, and it will make me very happy."

The child promised to do what she wanted. "You will find a parcel at the back of the top drawer, with your name written on it," continued the old woman, speaking with difficulty; "get it out and undo it."

The child obeyed, and found the parcel contained the clothes she wore on the day she was stolen, and on the top of which was neatly folded her little blue hood.

"I want to be buried in your little blue hood," said the old woman, "if you will let me; and I feel as if I could die easier, if I had it on my head. Get the scissors and let out the plaits; it will then fit me, as the gatherings above the cape are large and loose."

The little girl let out the hood, drawing out the blue ribbons, which made a little cloak of it, when she was in the habit of letting it fall over her pretty shoulder. In her nimble fingers it was but the labor of a few minutes. The old woman thanked her, and kissed her.

"Now, darling, call Peggy up, and get her to raise my head, while you put it on; then I shall be at rest."

The little widow was soon in the room, and raised the old woman's head as tenderly as she would have shifted an infant's on its pillow; while Edith put on the little blue hood, and tied it loosely under her chin.

"Now, promise," she said, taking Peggy's hand, "that it shall not be taken off when they come to lay me out."

The little widow burst into tears, and promised that no hand should touch her, saving her own and Little Blue Hood's, after she was dead.

"You will find more than enough to bury me," said the old woman, "in the green purse in the drawer, and it is my wish, and that of my darling—whom I shall soon part with for a little while—that you keep what remains for your kind attention to me. And now kiss me; for I am tired and sleepy."

They both kissed her; and she fell asleep, never to awaken any more on this side the grave.

CHAPTER XIX.

HOME.

THE good clergyman had visited the old woman numbers of times during her illness, and it is from the notes that he kindly supplied that we have compiled this work. They were partly taken down in pencil by her bedside, from the old woman's lips ; and partly written after he returned from visiting her, while the conversation they had together was fresh in his memory. The author regrets that the modesty of this really reverend gentleman is too great to even allow of his name appearing in connection with it. His object in taking such copious notes was, not only to apprise the parents of Little Blue Hood of all that had befallen the child from the day she was lost, but also to prepare them for her return home, after the old woman was buried. He said that the child expressed a strong wish not to see her parents until the grave had closed over the remains of the old woman, whom they could only look upon as an enemy, while she mourned her loss as a friend. Every day he sent by post a portion of the history of the Adventures of Little Blue Hood, so that, as he said, "When the happy hour of your meeting comes, she will have no tale to tell."

The worthy clergyman had received instructions from the parents of Little Blue Hood to become her banker ; and the first use she made of the funds he supplied her with, was to purchase mourning for Peggy and all her children, whom she wished to attend the funeral. It was soon known throughout the length and breadth of the old

Borough, that the pretty little street-hawker, they had all so much admired, was the daughter of a titled lady; and many a prophet rose up with a "I always said she was," and those who said so saw their prophecies fulfilled.

Through the interest of the worthy clergyman, and at the intercession of Little Blue Hood, the old woman was buried close to the foundation of St. Saviour's Church. He had taken the child out one day, to get a mouthful of fresh air, as he called it, beside the river, for she was pale and feverish through long confinement, and attending so closely on the poor old woman; and he then told her that Shakspeare and Johnson had been mourners in that old churchyard; also naming many of the great poets who were buried there. Then it was that Little Blue Hood expressed a wish for the old woman to be buried there; she hardly knew why she had such a wish, though it may be that she thought her own adventures might some day be numbered "among the tales that are told."

Such a funeral procession had not been seen in the old Borough for years, but it was to honor the living, and not to pay respect to the dead, that caused such a great mustering. All who had been customers to Little Blue Hood, though it had only been for a farthing's-worth of pins, a halfpenny reel of cotton, or a row of pearl buttons, were followers at that great funeral; where she, in all her childish beauty, was chief mourner; and, instead of a blue, on that occasion wore a sable hood, her sweet face shining in it like a star from out of the surrounding darkness.

It was the wish of the old woman that she should be borne to the grave on the shoulders of those she had known, in what she used to call "her better days;"

though, as she afterwards said to Peggy : "The best days of my ill-spent life have been my last, which the presence of our little angel has brightened."

The little widow had no difficulty in finding bearers, to carry her old mistress to the grave, who had known her in former years. They were all old and poor, and were richly rewarded for their attendance through the hand of the good clergyman, who acted as almoner to Little Blue Hood.

"Earth to earth, ashes to ashes, dust to dust; in sure and certain hope of the Resurrection to eternal life, through our Lord Jesus Christ."

The last solemn words are uttered, the earth has fallen with a strange, solemn, hollow sound on the coffin-lid, and she, that child mourner, stands motionless, looking down into the narrow bed, while her tears fall like rain on those remains, that will never know pain or sorrow any more.

When Little Blue Hood raised her eyes, red with weeping, they met those of her mother, who was standing on the opposite side of the grave—the grave of her who had so long divided them. A narrow plank had been left across the grave, after the coffin was lowered, and over this the child passed, to be folded in the embrace of her mother, who clasped her in speechless ecstasy, as she dropped on one knee, and held her to her beating heart, while her eyes were raised heavenward, and her lips stirred as if in prayer.

Had she passed triumphant over the grave of her enemy, or of her friend?

Trot was the first to discover the mother of his little mistress, and had gone to her during the reading of the solemn Burial Service.

After the lady had recognized and patted him—for she knew how his complexion had been changed, as well as her dear daughter's, through the long letter the good clergyman had written to her—he squatted down on the edge of the grave, and looked more sedate and full of thought than many of those who were there assembled.

The carriage was in waiting at the foot of London Bridge, and no sooner had the lady entered and seen her daughter seated by her side, than she uttered the word "HOME" to the footman, as he touched his hat to receive her commands. That word was passed to the coachman, who had already got Trot by his side on the box; for he had always been one of the dog's favorites. Trot had often been sentenced to ride with the coachman, whenever he had misconducted himself inside the carriage.

There are states of feeling which no written language can ever describe—which no tongue can ever give utterance to—such was the state of feeling in the heart of Little Blue Hood and her mother. To look into each other's eyes, to press their lips together again, to lie for a moment or two in each other's embrace, then to draw their faces apart, as if to be sure that the bliss they enjoyed was real: to utter only the words "my darling," and "my mother," is only to describe motion and sound. Their full hearts were laboring under feelings, which, in this state of existence, can never find utterance, and may be reserved for one of the delights of heaven; where, in their beatitude, the angels make known their love for one another. Who can tell?

Neither the heart of Little Blue Hood, nor that of her mother, could find words to express its feelings, as if there is a pleasure beyond any we can know while here, and which to partake of we must first die, and not until then be allowed to give utterance to the full expression of perfect love.

Inquire among the aged and the helpless, the poor and the needy, where Sorrow has alighted. and Misfortune found a pitiful home, and there you will near of a Ministering Angel, who is ever coming and going on errands of Charity, and Loving-kindness, and will be told that, in the days of her girlhood, she was known by the name of Little Blue Hood.

THE END.

www.ingramcontent.com/pod-product-compliance
Lightning Source LLC
Chambersburg PA
CBHW020032030726
47499CB00007B/2392